Max O'Rell

John Bull and his Island

Max O'Rell

John Bull and his Island

ISBN/EAN: 9783744729963

Printed in Europe, USA, Canada, Australia, Japan

Cover: Foto ©Andreas Hilbeck / pixelio.de

More available books at **www.hansebooks.com**

John Bull

and

his Island

BY MAX O'RELL.

TRANSLATED FROM THE FRENCH
UNDER THE SUPERVISION OF THE AUTHOR.

"C'EST ICY UN LIVRE DE BONNE FOY, LECTEUR."

Montaigne.

NEW-YORK:

CHARLES SCRIBNER'S SONS.

1889.

CONTENTS.

XII.

XIII.

XIV.

XV.

XVI.

XVII.

XVIII.

XIX.

vi CONTENTS.

John Bull and his Island.

I.

JOHN BULL is a large land-owner, with muscular arms, long, broad, flat, and heavy feet, and an iron jaw that holds fast whatever it seizes upon.

His estate, which he adds a little piece to day by day, consists of the British Isles, to which he has given the name of *United* Kingdom, to make folks believe that Ireland is attached to him ; the Channel Islands ; the fortress of Gibraltar, which enables him to pass comfortably through the narrowest of straits ; and the islands of Malta and Cyprus that serve him as advanced sentinels in the Mediterranean. When he has Constantinople, which he claims as his due, he will be satisfied with his slice of Europe. ?

In Egypt, he is more at home than ever ; in that country he can rest on his oars for the present. He took good care not to invent the Suez Canal ; on the contrary, he moved heaven and earth to try and prevent its being made. Yet behold him now, as a shareholder, casting his round covetous eyes upon it!

At the extremity of the Red Sea, at Aden, he can quietly contemplate that finest jewel in his crown, the Indian Empire ; an Empire of two hundred and forty millions of people, ruled by princes covered with gold and precious stones, who black his boots, and are happy.

On the West Coast of Africa, he possesses Sierra Leone, Gambia, the Gold Coast, Lagos, Ascension, St. Helena, where he kept in chains the most formidable monarch of modern times. In the South, he has the Cape of Good Hope, Natal, Zululand ; and he is *Protector* of the Transvaal. In the East, the Island of Mauritius belongs to him.

In America, he reckons among his possessions Canada, Newfoundland, Bermuda, the West Indies, Jamaica, part of Honduras, the Island of Trinidad, English Guiana, Falkland, etc.

Correctly speaking, Oceania belongs to him entirely. New Zealand is twice as large as England, and Australia alone covers an area equal to that of almost the whole of Europe.

With the exception of a few omissions, more or less important, such are John Bull's assets.

He has acquired all this territory at the cost of relatively little bloodshed ; he keeps it with an army considerably inferior in numbers to that of any of the other Great Powers, and partly composed of the refuse of society, in spite of which I am not aware that at the present moment any of John's possessions are the least in danger.

" But what shall it profit a man, if he gain the

whole world, and lose his own soul?" says Scripture. This is just what John Bull thought, and so in the other world he has knocked down to himself the kingdom of heaven—in his eyes as incontestably a British possession as India or Australia.

The French fight for glory ; the Germans for a living ; the Russians to divert the attention of the people from home affairs ; but John Bull is a reasonable, moral and reflecting character : he fights to promote trade, to maintain peace and order on the face of the earth, and the good of mankind in general. If he conquers a nation, it is to improve its condition in this world and secure its welfare in the next : a highly moral aim, as you perceive. "Give me your territory, and I will give you the Bible." Exchange no robbery.

John is so convinced of his intentions being pure and his mission holy, that when he goes to war and his soldiers get killed, he does not like it. In newspaper reports of battles, you may see at the head of the telegrams : "Battle of . . . So many of the enemy killed, so many British massacred."

During the Zulu war, the savages one day surprised an English regiment, and made a clean sweep of them. Next day, all the papers had : "Disaster at Isandula ; Massacre of British troops ; Barbarous perfidy of the Zulus."* Yet these excellent Zulus were not accused of having decoyed the English into a trap : no, they had simply neglected to send their cards to give notice of their arrival, as gentlemen

---

* You will still find in England people who will tell you that Nelson was *assassinated* at the Battle of Trafalgar.

should have done. That was all. It was cheating.
As a retaliatory measure, there was a general demand
in London for the extermination of the enemy to the
last man. After all, these poor fellows were only
defending their own invaded country. The good
sense of England prevailed, however, and they were
treated as worsted belligerents. England, at heart,
is generous : when she has conquered a people, she
freely says to them : "I forgive you." Above all
things she is practical. When she has achieved the
conquest of a nation, she sets to work to organize it ;
she gives it free institutions ; allows it to govern
itself ;* trades with it ; enriches it, and endeavours to
make herself agreeable to her new subjects. There
are always thousands of Englishmen ready to go and
settle in such new pastures, and fraternize with the
natives. When England gave her Colonies the right
of self-government, there were not wanting people
to prophesy that the ruin of the Empire must be the
result. Contrary to their expectation, however, the
effect of this excellent policy has been to bind but
closer the ties which held the Colonies to the mother-
country. If England relied merely upon her bayonets to guard her empire, that empire would col-
lapse like a house of cards ; it is a moral force,
something far more powerful than bayonets, that
keeps it together.

England's way of utilising her Colonies is not
our way. To us they are mere military stations

---

* Not only have the Colonies their own parliaments, but they
have their ambassadors in London, who, under the name of Agents-
General, watch over their interests. These Agents-General are
usually ex-ministers of the Colonies.

for the cultivation of the science of war. To her they are stores, branch shops of the firm "John Bull and Co." Go to Australia—that is, to the antipodes of London—you will, it is true, see people eating strawberries and wearing straw hats at Christmas: setting aside this difference, you will easily be able to fancy yourself in England.

The Spaniards once possessed nearly the whole of the New World; but, their only aim being to enrich themselves at the expense of their Colonies, they lost them all. You cannot with impunity suck a Colony's blood to the last drop.

It is not given to everyone to be a Colonist.

John Bull is a Colonist, if ever there was one. This he owes to his singular qualities,—nay, even to defects which are peculiarly his own.

It is this John Bull, this personage who plays so important a part in the world, and whom you meet in every corner of the globe, that we purpose observing at home.

II.

FOR making himself at home wherever he goes,
John Bull has a talent all his own. Nothing astonishes him, nothing stops him.* Cosmopolitan in
the highest degree, he is at his ease in the four
corners of the earth :

> " Laissez-lui prendre un pied chez vous,
> Il en aura bientôt pris quatre."

In a town in Normandy, where several English
families, attracted by the fine scenery around, have
taken up their abode, a doctor, a friend of mine,
offered his English patients the use of a large field
of his. This field had attracted their attention as
being nicely situated near the town, and just the
place for a game of cricket. Shortly after this act
of kindness, my friend received the following note :
"The members of the cricket club present their
compliments to Dr. H., and would be much obliged
to him if he would kindly get the potatoes, with
which half of *their* cricket field is planted, removed,

---

* " Nil admirari, prope res est una, Numici,
Solaque quæ possit facere et servare beatum."

as the ball is constantly getting lost among them."

"Possession nine points of the law." This is the principle of all annexations of territory. Let an Englishman settle in any out-of-the-way corner of the globe, and it will not be long before you see a Protestant church and a cricket field, the two first visible indications of an English Colony. The conquest of India was practically made by the East India Company, that is to say, by a few London merchants.

John Bull is proud, brave, calm, tenacious, and a consummate diplomatist.

Proud, he will never doubt of the success of his undertaking; brave, he will carry it through; calm, he will calculate with a cool head the material advantages of the victory; tenacious, he will know how to make it fruitful. Diplomacy answers for the rest.

The sentiment of his dignity is evinced in him at an early age, and national pride incites him to perform acts of heroism at an age when sweetmeats seem to be the chief attractions of life.

While I was at school in Paris, I remember a score of us schoolboys were one day gathered about the crossbeam of a gymnasium, jumping, one after another, on to a heap of sand. Among us was a young English boy, about twelve years old, watching eagerly for his turn. The poor child was suffering from hernia, and we tried to dissuade him from his purpose. "Why not?" said he: "you do it; why shouldn't I?" And in spite of all our entreaties, he mounted the crossbeam, sprang, jumped——but to

rise no more. We carried him to his bed. An hour
after, he had breathed his last. "It shall not be
said," he murmured in his death throes, "that an
Englishman cannot jump as well as a Frenchman."
Poor little hero! A few days before, we had all
done justice to the contents of a well-filled hamper
that his mother had sent him from Devonshire. He
had insisted upon our all tasting the nice things
that came from his home. Home! This is a word
that our language lacks. It is true we have *foyer ;*
but it is a word used chiefly in the elevated style,
while in England there exists not a man, however
lowly, but possessed of a heart to feel and love, who
is not a little moved by the word *home.* This may be
to a certain extent explained by the fact that every
Englishman has his own little house, and that the
climate, which does not foster open-air pleasures,
makes the intimate joys of the fireside better appreciated. Go and try to feel poetically inspired
over the subject of the domestic hearth, when you
live on a fifth-floor back !

M. de Chateaubriand, who was not above walking
in the steps of M. de la Palisse, has said somewhere
that, were it not for a certain sentiment, inborn in
man, that holds him to his country, his greatest
pleasure would be to travel. The Englishman forms
the best illustration of this *truism*, as our friend John
Bull would put it. He loves voyages, adventures,
dangers. A vast stretch of ocean, a cloud-capped
mountain, perilous ascents, voyages of discovery in
strange lands, thrill him with delightful emotions.
He is in his element.

Call the Englishman wild, eccentric,—mad, if you

will ; but to do great things one must not hesitate at straying from the beaten track. He will brave every conceivable danger in order to be able to say that he has climbed to the summit of Mont Blanc, or that he has been nearer the North Pole than any other explorer.

Obstinate as a mule, stubborn as a bull-dog, the difficulties in his path will but act as incentives to him. He has traced himself a programme : nothing will prevent his carrying it out. He leaves England with his diary written beforehand. He has settled to be at the top of a certain mountain at a certain time ; he is bound to be there : and I promise you that, if he has not rolled down some precipice, there you will find him. General Wolseley had announced to his countrymen that he would subdue Egypt in twelve days. He took fifteen. It was high time : John Bull was beginning to grumble.

I was walking one evening on the quay at Saint-Malo. It was blowing a furious gale. The Southampton boat had just started notwithstanding. Came two Englishmen breathless : "Where is the boat ?" they asked.

"Gone."

"Hail her: she is still in sight; we are bound to go!"

"Surely, gentlemen, you are joking."

"Well, then, can you get us a sailing boat to take us to Jersey ?"

"I have one," said a sailor ; "but the sea is very rough : I must charge you two hundred francs."

"Never mind : get her ready."

"But, gentlemen," cried the bystanders, "you will be ill, and endanger your lives."

"What's that to you ?" said they, with a contemp-
tuous glance at the crowd around.

The face of the younger man, a fine young fellow
of about twenty, beamed with delight at the idea of
the dangers he was going to brave.

It was useless reasoning longer : the fisherman set
out with them. A few moments later the frail barque
was under sail, now hidden from sight by a huge wave,
now reappearing, and making visible the tall form of
the young.man at the rudder. " *Vogue la galère,*"
said the spectators : "those English people are mad."

Every Englishman of good family can manage a
boat, drive a carriage, and is at home in the saddle.
Accustomed from his childhood to bodily exercise,
he thinks nothing of a hundred mile walk or a row
from London to Oxford. A walking tour from London to Edinburgh is not at all an uncommon thing
to hear of. The outfit of an English tourist is no
encumbrance to him : he puts into a bag a flannel
shirt, a dozen collars, and a couple of pairs of socks
and, stick in hand, off he goes. I know one who
walked last year as far as the north of Scotland.
His friends teased him for having made up his mind
to take the train to the border. "A little pluck,"
said they to him, "do the whole on foot while you
are at it, your railway ticket will destroy all the
merit and charm of the affair." The year previous,
during the summer holidays, he had walked a distance of over a thousand miles in Norway.

This habit of walking is kept up by Englishmen
to a very advanced age. Go to the provinces, you
may there see old men doing their five or six miles
every day ; when they knock off, it is to take to

their beds, and prepare to go and sleep in Abraham's bosom. In the country, in France, our old men, gouty or crippled with rheumatism for the most part, pass half the day at table ; after their dinner, you may see them leaning on the arm of an old servant, crawling along the public promenades. In France, a man is often old at sixty ; the effects of a youth, too often spent in dissipation, and of a life in most cases sedentary, become sadly apparent, and if he live to a great age, the closing years of his existence are a burden to himself and to those around him.

> " C'est une charge bien pesante,
> Qu'un fardeau de quatre-vingts ans,"

said Quinault ; but such is not the case in England : here every one dies of a green old age. I have an old friend in his eighty-eighth year, who, summer and winter, religiously takes his tub every morning, and who would not think of sitting down to luncheon without first having done his three or four miles. He is bright, cheery, will sing you a song at dessert, and never forgets to tell you of the peas he means to sow *next* year. Methinks he will gather many a bushel yet.

A young Oxford professor of my acquaintance undertakes, every year, in a small boat, a voyage that lasts from one to two months. He travels with his wife to the point of departure : there he hires a boat, places the lady at the rudder, and away goes the skiff. At night they put up at some riverside inn. Next morning, fresh provisions are put on board, and they are off again. They have seen in this way most of the lakes and rivers of Europe. Ingenuous and full of enthusiasm, it is a pleasure to hear them talk of their travels; and if I may be allowed to offer you a piece of advice, it is to read, as soon as it appears, a charming book which will have for title "ON THE RIVER."

Others go from one capital of Europe to another on a velocipede. Some young couples take their honeymoon trip on a double tricycle. They go through England from village to village without creating the least excitement. Here, one is used to eccentricity in all its forms. In this fashion, they avoid the wedding calls of the curious, and drink deep draughts of pure country air. These double tricycles bear the very appropriate name of *sociables*, and are admirably constructed for the honeymoon. I recommend you to try them. The two seats are placed closely side by side, so that hearts may overflow, hand press hand, and lips meet lips. Arrived at the top of the hill, you stiffen your body, bend your knees and fly like the wind to the bottom of the valley. The air through which you have sped gives you force to mount the next slope as easily as you climbed the last. This little pastime—to say nothing of woods by the way where you may rest, ramble, lose each other and find each other again,—all this, I say, has always appeared to me delightful. It is within the reach of all purses, and by such means a man may spare his sweet young companion the annoyance of commencing married life with butcher's and baker's bills, and other surprises that will recall her all too soon to the stern realities of this prosaic world, and all through life there will last the sweet recollection of that little trip—the uphill part especially.

III.

JOHN BULL only lifts his hat on grand occasions: for
instance, when he hears "God Save the Queen"
played or sung. Then he may be said to be saluting
his country, his Queen, his flag—himself if you like.

In the most fashionable shops, in his club, in Parliament even, he keeps on his hat.

I know a Frenchman who threw up his situation
because his employer did not return his bow.

In business, the Englishman throws overboard all
the formalities imposed by politeness. His style is
freezingly cold, and would appear to us almost rude.
He invariably terminates his letters "Yours truly."
And, after all, I scarcely see why, when we send our
creditor a cheque, it should be thought necessary
to beg him to accept the assurance of the extreme
respect with which we have the honour to sign ourselves his very humble and obedient servant. I prefer *Yours truly.* "Time is money."

Ask John Bull if you are in the right train for
such-and-such a place, you will get *Yes* or *No* for an
answer, and nothing more.

When he enters an omnibus or a railway carriage,

if he does not recognise any one, he eyes his fellow-
travellers askance in a sulky and suspicious way.
He seems to say, "What a bore it is that all you
people can't walk home, and let a man have the carriage comfortably to himself!" It must be admitted,
though, that the notices with the advice, "Beware
of pickpockets, male and female," which confront
him in these places, are quite enough to cool his gal-
lantry, be it said for his justification.

London omnibuses are made to seat six persons
on each side. These places are not marked out.
When, on entering, you find five people on either
hand, you must not hope to see any one move to
make room for you. No, here everything is left to
personal initiative. You simply try to spy out the
two pairs of thighs that seem to you the best padded,
and with all your weight you let yourself down between them. No need to apologise, no one will
think of calling you a bad name.

If you open the door to let a woman alight, she
will say, "Thank you" to you, if she be a lady. If
she happen not to be, you will get no thanks, and
should be only too happy if her look do not seem
to say, "Mind your own business."

At home and abroad each one for himself. There
are no omnibus offices where you must book. In
France, we do everything in a military style. The
Englishman, who is a better runner than his fellow-
creature, does not see why he should not have the
latter's place if he is nimble enough to catch it.
Competition open to all; the fittest will survive; it
is the motto of free-trade, and of the whole nation.

Outside his own house John Bull is not communi-

cative : he leaves his neighbour alone, and expects
to receive a like treatment at his hands. If you remark to an Englishman, in a smoking compartment
that he has dropped some cigar-ash on his trousers,
he will probably answer : " For the past ten minutes I
have seen a box of matches on fire in your back coat
pocket, but I did not interfere with you for that."

John Bull is absolute master in his own house,
which he calls his castle. If you present yourself
to him without an introduction, he will put his back
up and soon show you to the door as an intruder.

On the other hand, if properly armed with a letter
of introduction, you will find him hospitable, affable,
and unsuspecting, and you will readily become the
friend of the family.

It is impossible to admire too much the confidence
of the English even in business. Bureaucracy is unknown. You have not to produce your papers at
every moment. If you are a candidate for a place
of any kind, you simply send a copy of your testimonials. If you want to marry, you state your age,
and whether you are a bachelor or a widower, etc.
I repeat it, John Bull has quite shaken off the yoke
of red tape. A man who has lied before a tribunal
is prosecuted for perjury; a man who has deceived his
neighbour is kicked out of the house for his pains.

In the midst of this jostling crowd, all eager to
reach a certain goal, you must not mind a little
knocking about. Every man, English or not, who
has some ability, and determines to succeed, does
succeed. This is a country where, as an Englishman said to me once, "the sun shines for all alike."

I may add that it was but a figure of speech.

IV.

LONDON has five hundred and sixty-eight railway stations, and through Clapham Junction alone there pass thirteen hundred and seventy-four trains a day. These figures, which are official, do not include goods trains. The Metropolitan Company announced to its shareholders that between January 1st and December 31st, 1881, a hundred and ten millions of people had been carried over their lines. Steam has robbed travel of its poetry; but if we no longer live in days of heroic adventure, we may console ourselves with the thought that we live in days of ease and comfort. Go and ask an official at Clapham Junction to register your luggage, and you will get laughed at to your face. You merely put on your boxes your name and destination, get them labelled, and have them put into the luggage van. At your journey's end you point out your trunks to a porter, and that is all. No confusion; and I never met with any one who had lost the least luggage. In France, it would seem as if bureaucracy had been invented to give employment to the company's large number of servants.

Railway accidents are rare, marvellously rare,

when oi. thinks of those networks of railroads that are enough to make one's head swim to look at them.

Railway journeys are not always unattended by dangers, though. If you value your reputation in the least, never remain alone in a compartment with a woman. Even were she the owner of the loveliest pair of eyes, flee for your life to the next carriage. There are certain ladies in existence who levy black mail on a vast and somewhat fantastic scale.

A French diplomatist of my acquaintance was one day travelling alone with a woman, who appeared to him to be a lady in every respect. At the end of about half an hour, their eyes chanced to meet. The lady immediately smiled. Such an irresistible smile ! What bewitching eyes ! My friend smiled too. Nothing more. But he paid for it.

" Are we far from Cannon Street Station, do you know ? " said the charming lady.

" No, madam ; we shall be there in five minutes."

" Very well, sir ; if you do not hand me over twenty pounds this instant, I shall give you in charge at the station for having insulted me."

My friend paid : he was a wise man.

Such cases are very frequent.

I know a gentleman who detests the smell of tobacco, but who invariably travels with the smokers rather than run the risk of finding himself alone with a woman.

One day he had just taken his seat in a smoking compartment.

Up comes a lady to the door : " Smoking carriage, madam ! " cries he, scenting a lady in search of game.

" Oh ! I don't mind."

2

"That may be. *I* do though." And, at the risk of passing for a bear, he held on to the handle of the door, and remained master of the situation. Honour was safe : that was the main thing.

These charmers are not the only travelling companions to be shunned. One of the most to be dreaded is the old maid who takes up her position in front of you, and asks you point blank if you are prepared to meet your Maker. Her name is Christian-Worker, and she exercises her profession wherever she goes, distance is no object to her. Keep a sharp look-out : this one is not to be easily shaken off. She is of a persevering temperament, and difficulties do not daunt her. On the contrary, she rather likes them. The deeper dyed your sins, the greater she thinks is her merit in leading you back to the right path. As a rule, she waits to open fire until the train is going at full speed. Then she has you. No use trying to escape. You have only one alternative : either you must grin and bear it until you reach the next station, or else pitch her out of the window. You regret your want of courage to adopt the latter plan, which of course would send her straight to paradise to receive her reward. One of her favourite and comforting remarks (especially in a railway carriage) is: "Ah ! sir, should we not always be prepared to meet death—accidents come so unexpectedly ?" I succeeded one day in closing the mouth of one of these bores by saying, in broken English : "*Me not Anglish.*" "Oh !" sighed she, "what a pity !" and she left me alone. I recommend you the plan : it is the only safe and legal one I know of.

Over here, you are not locked up in a waiting-room until your train comes in. You roam where you like about the station, and your friends may see you off and give you a handshake as the .train leaves the platform.

The functionary is scarcely known. There are more of them at the station of *Fouilly les Epinards* than in the most important station in London. You see placards everywhere: "Beware of pick-pockets;" "Ascertain that your change is right before leaving the booking desk;" "Have your luggage labelled, and see that it is placed in the train." The Englishman does not like being taken in hand like a baby. He keeps his eyes about him, minds himself and his belongings, and you do the same. He makes no more of going to Australia than we of going to Passy; no fuss, no confusion. The question he asks himself on setting out for the change of air (doctors here will order you a voyage to Australia just as ours will tell you to try Saint-Germain or Vichy) is: "Shall I come home by way of China or San Francisco?"

His ticket taken, he instals himself in his berth, like a king in his castle.

In France, the Administration takes us under its wing. The Englishman does not like that kind of thing. He prefers to be let alone; he feels big enough to take care of himself.

I travelled once from Boulogne to Paris with a Briton, who snored away in his corner as happy as a king. Presently up came a most polite porter, who, waking him, inquired whither he was bound:

"Why do you wake me?"

"But, sir, I thought you would perhaps be obliged to me for waking you."

"Leave me alone ; I want to sleep. I have a right to : I have paid for my ticket."

"Of course you have, sir, but—— "

"Leave me alone, I tell you."

At Creil the train drew up ; my travelling companion wanted to alight."

"Take your seat, sir ; the train does not stop here."

"Yes, it does, I see ; I want to get out."

"But, sir, you will be left behind."

"That's nothing to do with you ; mind your own business. I want to get out. You are my servant."

Down he got, and did not reappear either. Great was my surprise, on arriving at Paris, to see my fine fellow upon the platform.

"Halloa !" I exclaimed ; "how did you get here ? "

"Oh ! I jumped into the luggage van," replied he.

Another time, at the Charing Cross station, a sturdy little fellow about twelve years old wanted to get into a train that was already in motion. Two porters pulled at him from behind to prevent him accomplishing his design. He does not hesitate long : he deals each of them a fine blow with his elbow, springs upon the step, jumps into the carriage, and shouts at them from the window : "I say, I didn't knock you down, you know, because there wasn't time, but don't try me again."

The trains are swift and the carriages excellent. This is the result of competition. You can go from London to Manchester by five different lines. Each company tries to obtain your patronage by offering you more advantages than the others. Plain wooden seats have disappeared from all third-class carriages, which are now better than second class ones in France, and one can travel third by express trains.

You go to a refreshment-room, help yourself, state what you have taken and pay. Just the same is done in the City restaurants at lunch-time. Gentlemen generally eat standing up : they are served on the instant ; there is no time to lose ; no serviettes—you wipe your mouth with your handkerchief. Lunch is despatched in ten minutes. You might almost hear a pin drop while this roomful of merchants, clerks, etc., are taking their mid-day repast.

On entering an office, the first thing you see written up is : " You are requested to speak of business only." It is the reign of steam.

You should see the City between nine and ten in the morning, when the railways and vehicles of all kinds are disgorging their swarms of busy bees. At four o'clock a calm begins to set in, and on Saturdays the City is deserted from two o'clock in the afternoon.

The docks, too, are well worth a visit, with their forests of masts. These are sights you will never forget.

Take a walk in the City, and look up in the air ; the telegraph wires are enough to make you believe that some gigantic spider has spun a web over your head.

For a penny you can send six sheets of letter paper by post to any part of the United Kingdom. There is an hourly delivery of letters in the City. I borrow the following lines from the excellent *Annuaire.*

Hamonet, Guide général des Français à Londres :—" In the E.C. district alone there are delivered every morning a million of letters ; and that which shows to what a degree the commercial life of the United Kingdom is concentrated in the metropolis, is the fact that the number of letters delivered within the postal district of London forms more than a fourth part of all the letters delivered in Great Britain. Scotland does not receive half as many letters as London, and Ireland not one-third. To give an example : one City house receives three thousand letters a day. This development of letter writing is all the more remarkable from the fact of the post having a serious competitor in the telegraph."

I cannot leave the City without saying a word on the subject of the Lord Mayor. The first magistrate of London is elected annually by the Corporation. He is installed on the 9th of November. This ceremony forms the occasion for a civic fête, as M. Prud'homme would call it, that reminds one of carnival time, and in which the Lord Mayor plays the part of the fatted ox. The procession sets out from Guildhall at noon to go and present the Lord Mayor elect to the judges at Westminster. It is preceded by soldiers, and about a dozen bands of music. All the City companies are represented and headed by their respective banners. Horses, and horsemen disguised as knights and musketeers, are borrowed of a circus proprietor, and I have even seen camels and elephants (also lent by the circus proprietor) taking part in the performance. The Lord Mayor draws up the procession. Cinderella never dreamed of a coach as gorgeous as the one that carries My Lord

Mayor elect to Westminster. The procession parades the City thus until about four in the afternoon.

At six the banquet takes place. This banquet stands conspicuous among others on account of the presence of the Ministers of the Crown, and of the political speech that the Chief of Her Majesty's Government is expected to deliver on the occasion.

The English are fond of their ancient customs, and the Lord Mayor's Show, which would be quite a success at our Hippodrome is not likely to die out just yet.

V.

AN English father is absolute master in his own house : something of the father of antiquity.

The English mother is only just shaking off her shackles. In Mme. de Staël's time she only appeared for a few moments in the drawing-room to offer a cup of tea to her husband's guests. Even in the present day her position in the family is only one of secondary importance. She has not the authority that a mother has in France, nor even as much as her own son. In the house of a widow the eldest son is master ; especially is this the case among the aristocracy, whose titles, with the inalienable property attached to them, go to the eldest son, and to him alone.

The word *lord* means in Anglo-Saxon *the one who procures the bread*, the master ; *lady, the one who serves it*, the servant.

A son never kisses his father, and only rarely his mother. He shakes hands, the effusion of the heart goes no further. An English son would be afraid of losing his dignity if he caressed his mother. In

France, our mother is the récipient of our tenderest caresses, our nearest and dearest friend. We tell her our secrets ; nay, even our little escapades.* She may pretend to be very cross, and say, "Get along with you, sir ; you are a disgraceful character ; I won't listen to any more." Don't you believe her.

Ah, darling old mother! how vexed she would be if we were to take her at her word. How she cajoles us, how she soon brings back the conversation to the same subject, so that she may hear a few more little risky confidences. How she makes believe not to be listening, while all the while she is not losing a word! And how she pretends to be dreadfully horrified! and how a good kiss wins her over in an instant. Sweet, gentle counsellor! what happy moments have we all passed at thy side when we were just becoming possessors of a downy moustache, that we twirled with pride.

The English language has no word for *fredaine*, perhaps the thing does not exist on this side of the Channel. The Englishman is either virtuous or an utter reprobate ; very often virtuous, perfectly virtuous. In this country there is no middle course ; contrasts strike you in every phase of life.

In English family life there is no intimacy, no openness of heart ; stiffness and reserve ; affection, but little love. Thanks to the devotion of the Frenchman for his mother, he is more lovable than the young Englishman, but he is also more effeminate ; the latter is more self-reliant, more independ-

---

* An Englishman speaks of his frolics to no one, not even his most intimate friend. Over here *péché caché est tout-à-fait pardonné.*

ent, more virile. In France, love and respect for
the mother are to be found in the lowest peasant or
workman, and even a vicious life will not completely extinguish these sentiments in him. He
avoids his mother when he is intoxicated; he dreads
her reproaches, shuns her scrutinising gaze. In
England he beats her, or turns her out of the house.
Let those who may doubt the exact truth of these
statements open any English newspaper and read for
themselves. The French workman would say to any
one who had insulted his mother, " Look here, say
what you like to me, but just let my mother alone,
will you !" For him the dear old woman is something sacred. Among us, a mother dies surrounded by the children who have tended her in her de-
clining years. Here, she works as long as her
strength lasts ; when she has become a useless piece
of furniture she goes to the Union and dies.

If among the well-to-do classes the mother is not
to be found in the foreground, it is mainly to the
fact of her entering upon married life portionless
that we must look, I think, for the explanation. The
dot gives to the French wife a certain feeling of independence and authority in the house. She is somebody, her husband's equal. In England, she is
something more than a housekeeper in point of
rank, but at the same time something less, if we consider that no wages are due to her, and that she cannot give notice to leave. Moreover, she is generally
devoid of that little talent of diplomacy that every
Frenchwoman is more or less possessed of : she has
not the influence of the woman over the man. Here
the husband requires but one thing of his wife : to

keep his house well, to serve his meals punctually, and to manage his domestic affairs economically. He calls her his partner,—a sleeping partner, if I might risk a *jeu de mots* in English.

Adultery is frequent in the higher classes, among the rich and idle ; very rare among the middle and working classes. I do not mention the lower populace of London : their life is that of dogs, as I say elsewhere.

"A married man," said an Englishman of some importance to me one day, "is very foolish to be unfaithful to his wife. Why on earth should one blight one's peace of mind ? Is not one woman as good as another ? " In nine divorce cases out of ten, the co-respondent is an officer in Her Majesty's service. An officer-and-a-gentleman, having nothing particular to do in time of peace, is fond of keeping his hand in by shooting over other people's preserves. The co respondent is not unfrequently a young groom, as one may see by the newspapers. This sample of co-respondent begins at the spur : it is not very far to the garter ; the path is very attractive, *que voulez-vous?* Between the 1st of July, 1882, and the 1st of January, 1883, I counted seven cases of these favoured young flunkies in the newspapers. How many must there be still enjoying their good fortunes on the quiet !

Death is an event that astonishes no one, which the Christian neither fears nor dreads, and which in England consequently calls for few tears. "Was he insured ? " is a question asked upon the death of a father. "Yes ? Well, you see, we must all die sooner or later. God has called him home, and it should make you rejoice." The worthy fellow is buried, and soon forgotten. English cemeteries are deserts : here people have not the respect—I do not hesitate to call it love—that we feel for the dead. The Protestant Church does not pray for the dead ; she denies the doctrine of purgatory. To pray for the repose of a dead person's soul would be to doubt God's justice, to dictate to Him what He should do in the other world. The Englishman is serious and sensible in business matters ; he does not believe that a three and sixpenny mass is going to send his relative to Heaven. Our worthy mothers pay their money, and those that are not firm believers merely say to themselves, " Poor soul ! if it does him no good, it can do him no harm. After all, it is but three and six."

A son writes to his parents : " I am about to be married," or " I am married."

"We are glad to hear it," answer the parents; "we shall be happy to make the acquaintance of your wife."

But it is in Scotland above all that one must look for sound business principles. Indeed, those who have never been to Scotland cannot form a notion of what it is to be serious. A young Scotch friend of mine, of high literary reputation, generally spends, once a year, a month with this family on the outskirts of Edinburgh. His father is a Presbyterian minister occupying a very enviable position. On the day of his departure, my friend invariably finds on the breakfast table, by the side of his plate, a little paper carefully folded. It is a detailed account of the meals he has had during his visit to

his father's house : in other words, his bill. But
the son is as sound a Caledonian as papa, and
does not part with his coin before he has ascertained
that all the items are accurate, and the addition
correct.

"Why, father, I see you have marked bacon and
eggs for my yesterday's breakfast ; I assure you I
did not touch the eggs."

"You were wrong not to do so then, my boy :
they were on the table ; why didn't you help yourself ? "

I know another interesting Scotch papa who presents his children, as they come of age, with the
bill of all that he has spent upon them, including
the fees of nurse and doctor. The children sign and
undertake to repay the outlay.

The mother-in-law is not an object of terror in
England. Not being mistress at home, it would
never occur to her to impose her authority in her
son-in-law's house. "If you have to choose," says
M. Victorien Sardou, "between living with your
mother-in-law and shooting yourself, never hesitate:
shoot her." If your mother-in-law falls overboard,
it is an accident ; if she is fished out alive, we call
it a misfortune. To get rid of a mother-in-law,
people here do not have recourse to such extreme
measures ; diplomacy is called into requisition. I
recommend the following plan to young married
men : it proved a great success in the case of a
friend of mine. Awhile after the marriage, his
mother-in-law arrived and installed herself in his
house. My friend lavished the most assiduous
attentions upon her. He was not a church-goer,

but he went now to have the pleasure of carrying
the excellent lady's books of devotion. When a
walk was taken, it was to her that his arm was
offered. In the evening, after his wife had retired,
he sat up with his mother-in-law, and took a hand
at *besique*. At the end of a week, the mamma-in-
law vanished as if by magic. The young wife had
managed the matter.

When a Greek or Roman bride arrived at the
threshold of her new home, the bridegroom, taking
her in his arms, carried her to his hearth to offer a
sacrifice, and to eat with her the *panem farreum*.
This ceremony was intended to simulate carrying off
by force. Something analogous is practised in England as the bride leaves her parents' house. When
the wedding breakfast is nearly over, the friends
take up their position at the door of the house, and
lie in wait for the young couple. Their appearance
is the signal for cheers ; and then down falls on their
heads, in their necks, on their backs, a shower of
rice, and of all the old slippers that are to be found
in the house. Parents, friends, guests, servants,
neighbours, all join in the fun. On the part of the
parents, this old custom means : "Ah! rascal, you
are taking away my daughter! there, take that!"
On the part of the friends and the busy-bodies of the
neighbourhood, it means : "Ah! you wolf! you are
stealing a lamb from the fold! there, take this!"
Of course the origin of this custom must be looked
for a little further. The rice is the symbol of plenty,
and the old slippers the symbol of good luck. You
must turn up your collar and shelter yourself as best
you can against this hailstorm that beats upon you

from all sides, and jump into the carriage that is waiting for you.   Crack goes the whip ! off for the honeymoon ! and you have richly earned it.

After marriage the young Athenian or Roman wife was completely severed from her own family.   She lost her family rights, even her gods, which she exchanged for those of her husband.   In England, the young married woman is no longer at home in her father's house ; she goes there on a visit, and all are glad to see her, but she is no more one of the inner family circle.   Visits are counted.

It is a common mistake, generally made in France, to believe that primogenitureship exists in England. Quite on the contrary, there is nothing to prevent a man from making his will exactly as he pleases. Birthright exists only in the aristocracy.   The real estates of the nobility are attached to the title and are inalienable.   Yet noblemen can dispose of their personal property as may seem good to them.   As a rule, their lives are insured for fabulous sums, which, at their death, are divided among their children or other devisees.   Moreover, the younger sons are not to be pitied : they occupy the most lucrative positions in the army, the church, and the diplomatic and other civil services in the country and the Colonies.   A nobleman, on his deathbed, recommends his younger sons to a grateful country, which does not forget them.

VI.

ENGLISHWOMEN are remarkable for their fresh complexions, their decided and fearless gait, and the length of their feet, which reminds one that twelve inches go to the foot in England. Impossible to make *faux pas* with such bases as these. They cannot lose their centre of gravity.

When they are pretty, Englishwomen have no equals upon earth—they are angels of beauty ; but, too often, their faces have no expression, their eyes lack lustre and piquancy, their teeth are long and protruding, and when they laugh, they show their gums like a rhinoceros. They have only the beauty of youth. An Englishwoman is seldom handsome after thirty. The lower-class women of London are thin-faced or bloated-looking. They are horribly pale ; there is no colour to be seen except on the tips of their noses.

Their sculptural lines (generally straight ones) are suggestive, pronounced, exaggerated, or suppressed, according to the fashion of the day.

In 1879, it became fashionable to display a protr:berant corsage. There was not a woman, even the thinnest, that was not in a position to exhibit a bust that would have been a splendid capital to a Burgundian wet-nurse. In shop windows might have been seen twin gutta-percha balloons, or bags of millet-seed, which were sold under the name of *figure improvers.*

The esthetic movement has caused all these ridiculous deformities to disappear as if by enchantment.

In 1881, every one began to worship the beautiful. To be in good form, one had to become intense, appear to be dying of decline; therefore to be lean and pale, to have one's eyes encircled with black and lost in ethereal regions. The supreme object was to look consumptive. Walking was abandoned for a kind of crawl; ordinary meals were suspended, a little sustenance was taken; voices became deep and hollow; the face was made to express disgust for the reality of the world's pursuits. As in the time of Mascarille, the only adverbs employed were *consummately, utterly, terribly, supremely.* These lunatics would remain hours in ecstatic contemplation of a lily or an old cracked china tea-pot; they had become *terrible* geese, *consummate* idiots.

The female esthete wore her hair cropped, and her dress was of sombre tint and fifteenth century design. The male esthete, on the contrary, let his locks grow long, and looked, at a glimpse, as if he wore a chignon. The manners of the sexes were similar: the same limpness, the same gait, the same play of features. The upper part of the face had to be raised, so as to round the eyes and make the eyebrows disappear under the hair, while the lower jaw

3

was allowed to droop. The ideal to aim at was the expression of the gasping carp. A long sigh was drawn between each syllable ; consonants were pronounced as indistinctly as possible, and vowels were lengthened into long diphthongs. Stare as hard as you can, stick an eyeglass in your eye, put an ounce of treacle in your mouth, now look at yourself in the looking-glass and try to speak : you will see an esthete.

A few years earlier you might have seen all the ladies who prided themselves upon following fashion's lead walking lame. The reason was a slight lameness of the Princess of Wales, who had recently recovered from an attack of rheumatism.

These remarks are offered simply in answer to an assertion, often made, that the women of England are more serious than their French sisters. When ladies have no house to keep, no children to bring up, or no husband to follow, I will admire them as much as you please ; but I shall always hold them capable, when they like, of a little frivolity.

In many respects the Englishwoman is superior to the Frenchwoman : she is more natural ; she is less subject to vapours, and does not regularly get her *migraine*. She is not so naïve as the young French girl ; but, on the other hand, she is less childish. She goes out without her mamma or her maid, gives you a hearty grasp of the hand, and looks you unblushingly in the face. Unmarried, free as the air, she may go to a theatre, take a walk or even a journey with male companions ; she is the leader of society, indispensable at all social gatherings and pleasure parties. Married, she does not boast of leading her husband by the nose ; she attends to her house and children ; she does not make love to her husband, but neither does she make love to other men. If she is not more demonstrative towards the former, it is, in a great measure, his own fault : he permits no liberties to be taken with him. The Englishman has not the bump of amativeness ; his neck, on an average, does not measure more than fourteen inches ; her enticing ways would be entirely lost upon him. In her dignity, the Englishwoman refrains from making advances towards her lord and master for fear of their not being met with approval.

In France, after church on Sundays, we are accustomed to see young girls going to the public promenade to show their little new shoes. Their eyes are bent on the ground, they walk with little jerky steps ; it is a little exhibition. Mamma whispers on either side : " My daughter will have a hundred thousand francs for her *dot.*" These public Sunday walks, in country towns, always remind me of a fair at which the mothers trot out their daughters for inspection. No long, free, health-giving country walks there. No ! The roads are muddy, and the damp would penetrate the little delicate boots, and the pointed heels, intelligently fixed almost in the centre of the sole, are not calculated to encourage walking ; besides, who would there be to notice the silk dresses and fifty-franc hats ?

Now look at the young English girl, with her hair knotted simply on her neck ; she wears a sixpenny straw hat, which she has turned up on one side, a cotton dress, and strong-soled, low-heeled boots Racket in hand, see her setting out with some young fellows, and a troop of other girls as simply dressed as herself, to go to some distant field and play a game of lawn-tennis. Not one mamma in the party. On her return home she devours her dinner without shame.   What she values above gracefulness is health.   It is no compliment to say to an English girl : "You eat like a little bird ;" it would be a re- proach.   You will see the prettiest eat cheese and heartily crunch a stick of raw celery.

Summer and winter the English woman takes a cold bath every morning : whence her fresh com- plexion, her vigour, and her resplendent look of health.

A young girl of fifteen travels alone.   I know some who come thus to School in London from the north of Scotland.   In France, a young lady would not go without her maid to buy herself a pair of gloves in a shop on the opposite side of the street. I remember I was one day sitting in the Champs Elysées with two English ladies.   Beside us was a young French girl with her father and mother.   The person on the right of papa rose and went away, and we heard the young innocent say to her mother : "Mamma, may I go and sit by papa ?"   It was a baby of about eighteen or twenty.   Those English ladies laugh over the affair to this day.

With us a too strict watch over our children, and the fear of giving them too much liberty, engender a love of the secret and mysterious.   Everything in an English education tends to make young people self-reliant.   No mother or governess would think of opening a letter addressed to her daughter or pupil ; the girl has her private correspondence as sacred as that of her elders. No letters received on the sly ; no letters written to young sweethearts at midnight. The absence of suspicion destroys the charm of mystery. It is the Bartholos that make the Rosines ; and, alas, the Rosines that become Countess Almavivas. Virtue springs, blooms, and ripens beneath the generous rays of liberty and confidence.

The English girl has not her modesty shocked at every turn. She can buy a book or paper and read them . . . . without having her eyes opened. She has no need to hide her novel under her pillow ; she can read it in the drawing-room before her friends. The comic papers are written for her as well as for others. I take this to be the result of the liberty of the press ; public opinion is the best of censors. When one looks at the comic papers of France, one is tempted to ask one's self whether the *cocotte* and the adulterous wife are the heroines of French society.

Gentlemen never use objectionable expressions among themselves, nor indulge in risky jokes in the company of ladies.

In fact, everything in this country seems to foster the freedom that women and girls possess. In a railway station you will see written up over the door of a comfortable and well-furnished room : " Ladies' Waiting-room." In France it is simply, *Côté des dames ; Côté des hommes.* In Germany, it is still better : " Men ;" " Women." In Brittany, it is sublime ; there is no distinction.

Pride, which is eminently an English virtue, engenders sentiments of independence even in young girls. Daughters of good, well-to-do families, fre. quently take situations in offices, paint on china, or go out as governesses to earn their own pocket money. Others prefer to go to Canada, India, or Australia, as ladies' companions, rather than live an idle life at home. Besides, in English families, which frequently number from six to a dozen children, the daughters are portionless, and their matrimonial chances are far greater abroad than in their mother-country. So many of the younger men of the country have emigrated, that women are wanted in the Colonies, and England has too many.

The girls of the middle classes, I have said already, have no *dot;* or, if some have, it is the exception, and not the rule. A suitor, who said to a father, "What marriage portion shall you give to your daughter?" would be promptly and ignominiously dismissed from the house. When a man takes a wife, he is supposed to be able to provide for her. But a man is not at all bound to wait until he is in a good position in order to propose for a wife. No. I know young students who are engaged to young ladies, whom they will marry as soon as their incomes will permit. In some cases, the engagement lasts for years. The accepted lover is received in the family of the lady, who, in her turn, is personally introduced by him to his friends; and he is freely allowed to take her to parties and theatres.

English custom permits so much liberty to the young affianced couples that neither party is allowed by the law to withdraw from the engagement without the consent of the other. A woman may sue the lover who has forsaken her for damages.

When a young French girl has been engaged to be married and the engagement falls through, there is no harm done : the young people have only met in the company of their friends. But in England the case is different ; for years, perhaps, the lovers have been in the habit of taking sentimental and more or less solitary walks together. The young English-woman who has been engaged is a flower whose bloom has been a little rubbed off, and in the eyes of other men she has lost some of her value. So if her lover leaves her without a cause, the law allows her compensation in the form of damages. The accounts of breach of promise cases are the delight of ladies. And, indeed, some of them are exceedingly amusing. The love letters are all read aloud in court. The young plaintiff lays at the feet of the jury all the vows and kisses she has received. Some-times it is a sweet maid of forty, all broken-hearted, pleading her cause against a faithless lover who has forsaken her for a younger, prettier, or richer bride. Another time it is some young schemer, robbed of his dearest hopes, who sees a nice little fortune slip-ping from his grasp, and comes to ask the court to make him some compensation for the wrong done to his innocence and candour. I remember one who asked considerable damages because, said he, he had given up a good situation in order to live quietly with his future wife upon the income she possessed. I know one Englishman who was con-demned to pay five hundred pounds to a young girl for having neglected to carry out his promise of marriage. A month later, he led her to the altar— to get back his money.

Nothing is easier than to get married in England; no papers to produce, no consent to obtain ; a declaration, witnessed by two persons, to make before the registrar, and that is all.

A girl goes out one fine morning to post a letter, and, on her return, informs her parents that she is married. Thus does she act, if she is above one-and-twenty and her parents throw obstacles in the way of her getting married.

The husband of an unfaithful wife is not an object of ridicule in England ; he has only to prove adultery on the part of his wife to obtain a divorce. If the lover be a rich man, the husband does not fight a duel with him ; not so romantic, not so stupid ! He sues him for damages in proportion to the injury and annoyance he has sustained. When the lady is a woman of fortune, the damages granted sometimes amount to a fabulous sum of money, and the husband is on the laughing side.

Just as neat and clean as are the women of the middle and working classes, just so ignoble and filthy are the woman of the lower class. It is the lowest step of the social ladder. These creatures wear no linen. They are covered with a few loathsome rags ; their faces are haggard, dirty, and sullen-looking, or bloated by gin-drinking ; they have at least one black eye, dirty hair that has never felt the comb, and to crown the whole, an old battered bonnet *trimmed* with feathers, flowers and lace. Such feathers ! such flowers ! such lace !

The old women especially are a sight not to be forgotten ! They do not go to the workhouse, because there they would have to work, and they prefer to be free and die of starvation in the gutter. You may count these poor degraded wretches by hundreds of thousands in London alone. The young ones will not go out into service : they prefer working in manufactories, or, more frequently, selling matches, flowers, or worse still they find their living in the open air, in the streets, or in the parks. The immorality of these girls is revolting. Some of them appear to be rather pretty ; but how could you form an opinion of them without soaking them in warm water a few days ? These brazen-faced creatures may look from time to time with envy at the neat, smart, fresh-looking little housemaids who answer the door in the houses of the well-to-do classes ; but they dread the yoke. It is always the story of the Wolf and the Dog. They had rather want for everything, and keep what *they* call their independence. Respectable servants all come from the country.

That which strikes a foreigner in France is the simplicity and neatness of the women of the lower classes. Our peasant women, with their snowy caps, their open faces, that tell their own tale of a peaceful life and honest work, fill them with astonishment. These same women are the fortune of France ! All our worthy country girls without exception have their dozen or two of linen to take with them to service. In England, in London especially, they are brought up to consider themselves quite as good as ladies: whence the *trimmed* hats and finery . . . . . but no chemise.

Some go to the altar "when they have pressing reasons for it," said a clergyman of the Church of England to me one day. As a rule, they content themselves with the altar of Nature : it is the life of the lower animals.

The London flower-girl forms a curious subject of study for those whose ideas of flower-girls are founded upon Alexandre Dumas' description of them in his novels : innocent doves to whom the *roi Vert-Galant** did not disdain to throw and give kisses.   The voice of the London flower girl has the hoarseness of the drunkard's ; she exhales a stench of gin and dirt, and swears like any Norman carter.   When you take a rose from her basket, you throw her a penny, taking great care to keep at a respectful distance.   I remember to have seen, in 1869, on the course at Longchamps, the Princess of Metternich shake hands with Isabelle.   O Isabelle ! the London flower-girl has nothing in common with thee but her colour !

---

* Henry IV. of France.

VII.

ENGLAND is the home of shoddy. Thanks to free-trade, you can have a cardboard villa for two hundred pounds, and a silk umbrella for one and six. I don't wish to speak disrespectfully of free-trade : there is a reverse side to every medal, and the quality must often suffer from this mad rage for buying in the cheapest market. Thanks to free-trade, however, you can buy a pound of sugar here for threepence, while in France it is still sold at eight pence, in order that a few refiners may make rapid fortunes. Here no one would think of telling the sun to hide his face so that the candle makers might make their fortunes in half the time.

The houses are built with half-baked bricks, without a single stone. These houses are only intended to stand for ninety-nine years, after which they become, by right, the property of the free-holder. It is like placing money in the sinking fund. In sixty years time, half London will be rebuilt. I say *London*, because in the provinces the ground generally belongs to the owner of the house, who therefore employs better materials.

Punch, whom it is always useful to consult upon
these matters, represents an alarmed tenant, who
has just sent for his landlord, and is showing him
the dining-room wall, which has given way. The
poor landlord cannot make it out ; but all at once,
striking his forehead, he exclaims : " I'll bet some
body has been a leanin' agin it ! "

Windows and doors close badly. It is in vain that
you make a fire and sit in front of it : your back
freezes. I have heard serious Englishmen declare
that houses would be unhealthy without these
draughts. After all, this is very possibly true ; for
the bricks of which they are built must contain foul
gases, which can thus partly escape through the
chinks of the windows and doors.

There are few houses which do not show signs of
damp inside. " It rains indoors, here," I said one
day to my landlord.—" Well, umbrellas are cheap
enough," he replied.

Once I went to a ready-made boot shop, and
bought a pair of patent leather boots, for, I am
bound to admit, the modest sum of eleven and
sixpence. I was going to a ball in the evening.

After dancing for about an hour, I felt the sole
of my foot getting delightfully cool. Gliding
carefully, I left the drawing-room to go and seek
out the cause of this unexpected treat. I soon
discovered that while the upper part of my boot
faithfully stuck to its position, the lower part, sole
and heel, had become transformed into a sandal.

Indignant, I went next day to the shopkeeper,
and produced the offending boot. At first he
appeared quite astonished.

"What can you have been doing with these boots?" he asked me.

" Why, dancing in them, of course," I replied.

"Oh, well," cried he, " that's *where* it is."

Moral : Pay thirty shillings a pair for your boots; they will be cheap at the price.

When you have bought all you require in a shop, you place your piece of gold on the counter. The shopkeeper takes it up, sounds it on a metal plate to be sure that it is good, and hands you your change.

You, on your part, try all the silver he gives you. "You took me for a rogue; I take you for another : we are quits; I forgive you."

Under the present system of education, the shopkeeping class is not likely to improve. In former times a shopkeeper loved the shop where his forefathers had honourably carried on business, and he was as proud of the signboard over his door as the Montmorencys of their escutcheon. Even in the present day, in France, he brings up his family in the shop, and his wife is not ashamed to sit behind the counter and keep his books. In England, the wife and daughters of the shopkeeper are *ladies ;* they play the piano, and go about in furs and gold chains to display the large profits of papa. The son seldom succeeds his father : the business is sold to one of the shopmen.

Read the announcements of the tradespeople, and you will see that they are all celebrated. Their articles are known all over England, famous throughout Europe, or the best in the world. If you go to a chemist or perfumer, and ask him

whether he keeps Farina's Eau de Cologne, or any
other well-known article of pharmacy or perfumery,
he will invariably reply : " Yes, we have the article
you name ; but if you will try our own, you will
find it far superior."

The most insignificant apothecary has his own
tooth-pastes, and washes for promoting the growth
of the hair, or for imparting to the complexion the
lustre of youth, all of them of his own make. He
prefers selling these articles, because he knows
what they cost him, whilst upon well-known preparations he can only make a modest profit.

The London public, tired of paying outrageous
prices to the tradespeople, has organised co-operative societies all over the metropolis. People joined
together, took premises, and stocked them with merchandise procured wholesale. Companies soon followed, all founded upon the same principle, and at
the end of a few months only, most tradesmen put
up the following announcement in their shops :
" Things sold here at co-operative prices." What is
certain is, that articles of every-day use have diminished in price since the establishment of this formidable competition. I used to pay eight shillings a
bottle for a tonic that I have been taking regularly
for years. I now get this medicine made up at the
stores of which I am a member, and it costs me
three shillings : it is still two shillings profit for the
druggist ; but I grumble no more.

I know a sharper who has put up over his door :
" For a shopkeeper, honesty is the best policy."
His shop is besieged on Saturday nights.

In one of the City streets may be seen two um

brella makers' shops side by side. The master of
one has written up on a red board : "If you do not
wish to be disappointed, you must buy your umbrella here." His neighbour displays a blue board,
on which is written in golden letters : "If it is a
really good umbrella that you want, look sharp ; my
shop is the place where you will find it."

Every grocer—I might say without exception—
displays the following announcement in his shop :
"When you have once tasted our tea, you will drink
no other." One of the largest tea-houses is not
ashamed to publish the following advertisement in
all the public thoroughfares and railway stations of
England. "We sell at three shillings a pound the
same tea as we supply to dukes, marquises, earls,
barons, and the gentry of the country." The poor
viscounts are left out : it is a regrettable oversight.

The English are better traders than manufacturers. The article they produce has no finish, no
elegance. The French workman is an artist in his
way ; the work of the English artisan is purely
manual, and he only turns out substantial things.

As agents, the English are not to be surpassed.
This kind of business was first started by the Jews.
They prefer being agents and brokers to being
manufacturers ; it gives them an opportunity of
plundering two Philistines—the producer and the
consumer.

Fabulous sums are spent in advertising. The
Times has more than sixty closely printed columns
of advertisements every day. Some firms advertise
in every newspaper and railway station throughout
the kingdom, and on the cover of every book and

periodical that appears. These advertisements are often *cautions*, indeed, the public should take them as *avertissements*. Judge for yourself: I will give you two or three.

"It will soon be considered a crime in the eyes of the law to have allowed a patient to die without having given him a dose of Eno's (so he does) Fruit Salt. Sold at 2s. 9d."

"To let, a Journalist, by the week or month. Will supply articles on travels, biographies, and essays." This advertisement appeared in the *Athenæum*, the best English literary paper. Again: "Upon receipt of a stamped envelope will be sent the photograph of a baby before and after taking Dr. Ridge's Food."

The best advertisements are those that promenade the streets in a file. These poor devils, forsaken of God and man, that carry two boards, one on the chest and one on the back, have been aptly named "sandwiches."

I was walking one day in Fleet Street, when, to my great astonishment, I saw pass a dozen fellows with shaved heads and dressed in convicts' uniform. They were accompanied by a warder. "It is shameful," said I to a friend at my side, "that those poor creatures should not be taken away in a van." They were chained in couples, and on their backs a large "14" was visible. It was the advertisement of a vaudeville named "Fourteen Days," and which was being played with success at the Criterion Theatre at the time.

At the windows of all fashionable shops you see: *Ici on parle français.* The indefinite pronoun *on* generally refers here to the person who happens to be out when you enter the shop. I speak from experience.

The spirit of business in England has reached its highest pitch. I know a north country shipowner who sold his sailing vessels to his sons, and then competed with them with steamers.

When you pay a railway fare you can, at the same time, by paying threepence extra, have an insurance ticket. If an accident should happen and you were killed, the company would pay to your heirs the sum of a thousand pounds. I know an Englishman who never fails to provide himself with a ticket of this sort. "Every time I reach my destination safe and sound," said he to me one day, "would you believe it? . . . . I feel a little bit disappointed."

There is not a man who lifts his hat as a funeral passes through the streets. In this country you must be useful in order to inspire esteem or respect, and a dead person is not useful. I know nothing more saddening than the sight of an English funeral. They manage these things better in Ireland. At any rate, they manage them more gaily ; they all get drunk at the funeral of a relative or friend.

John Bull, good patriot as he is, prefers a British article to any other. When he is obliged to keep one of dubious quality, he baptizes it with a foreign name. We are all the same, for that matter. What we French call "the Neapolitan disease" is the same as that which the Italians call "the French disease." The Germans seem, in England, to have obtained

4

the preference.   The adjective *German* seems to be in English synonymous with *bad*.   German silver and German sausages are articles that I would not recommend to my bitterest foe.

To go away without saying good bye is called in English "to take French leave."

The Spanish word *hablàr*, which means " to speak," gave us the French word *habler*, which means "to speak boastfully."   The Spanish have taken their revenge : "to speak boastfully" is, in their language, *parlàr*.   Take that !

VIII.

M. GUIZOT tells us that Alfred, to put the honesty of
his subjects to the test, used to cause bracelets of
gold to be hung up in public places. They were
never stolen, and if a traveller dropped his purse by
the roadside, he had no need to turn back and seek
it, for he was certain to find it untouched, even
though he did not pass that way again for a month.

Such was the Saxon in the time of Alfred the
Great. *Quantum mutatus ab illo!* How the railway
has changed him! I maintain that a London shopkeeper would consider himself dishonoured if he did
not give false weight ; that a railway booking clerk
would go and hang himself if he could not rob you of
a shilling out of the change of a sovereign; that an
omnibus conductor would not keep to his occupation
a month if he could not double his wages by cheating the company or the passengers ; that no cab-
driver ever in his life demanded the right fare, and
has even very rarely accepted it ; that no blind beggar ever said "Thank you," before having made
sure with his own eyes that the coin offered to him
was a good one.

My wife came home one day disconsolate. "What do you think?" she said to me, "I gave a two-shilling piece to the omnibus conductor, and I find he has given me two and three-pence change. Fancy, poor fellow! perhaps the father of a family, and he will have to make up the sixpence to the company out of his own pocket." I was just going to mingle my lamentations with those of my wife, when it occurred to me to ask her to let me see the florin in question. "Console yourself," said I, after having examined it; "the children of the poor fellow will have a good time to-morrow." The florin was a bad one.

The first wedding present that an English mamma gives a married daughter is a pair of scales. Every mistress of a house knows that it is necessary to weigh all provisions, and continue to change trades-people until one has ascertained which of them gives the nearest approach to proper weight.

It would be very wrong to apply to all the trades-people of England the remarks which I have just made about the lower-class ones of London. In the country, I have always found them to be polite, upright, and of an education that I might almost call superior.

In England, you must before all things be successful. No one pities the man who is down, he is shunned and ridiculed. He is called a lazy fellow or a fool; you may choose which you prefer to be. The aristocrat and the rich man, such are the Englishman's two idols. John Bull, upon his deathbed, invariably says to his heir: "My son,

get money, honestly if you can ; but get money." *
Here, more than anywhere,

> "*La vertu sans argent est un meuble inutile.*"

Nothing succeeds like success, runs the English
proverb. That signifies, in good plain English,
that the end justifies the means, and that if you
have kept within the law in building up your
fortune, very few people will question you as to the
means by which you attained your object. *Legal*
and *loyal* are doublets, says the philologist. Alas !
so they are ; *loyal* is the good old popular form ;
legal is a word of recent and learned formation,
with a signification suited to the exigencies of
modern civilization.

Become a rich man in England, and you will have
acquired every good quality, nay, every talent. You
may patronise the arts, govern the public schools, be
Member for the University of Oxford, Member of
the House of Lords even. "A man of wealth is
dubbed a man of worth." It is Pope who has said it.

Poverty is no vice in France. It is in England.

But everything has its redeeming point. This
thirst for wealth, this adoration of the golden calf,
has made the English nation a nation of bees.
Everyone works. The heir of a millionaire does not
dream of a life of idleness. The Duke of Argyle,
whose eldest son is the husband of one of the
Queen's daughters, has another who is established
in Liverpool as a tea merchant. Our country lord-
lings would think they were lowering their dignity

---

* . . . . . . rem,
si possis, recte ; si non, quocumque modo, rem.

in contributing to the prosperity and wealth of the nation. In their uselessness, they prefer vegetating upon a few hundred francs a year, passing their time at *écarté* in their clubs, running into debt, and borrowing a small sum to enable them to present their parish church with a stained-glass window, that shall hand down to posterity the glorious name of an ever parasitical family.

Give fifty thousand francs to a Frenchman, and he will place them in the funds and retire from active life. Give the same sum to an Englishman, and he will either spend it in a month, or go to the colonies and turn farmer. It is all or nothing with him. Fifty thousand francs! In English money that makes but two thousand pounds! What a meagre sum! How small it sounds to the ear of an Englishman!

In landed property alone the Duke of Devonshire has a fortune which amounts to about eight millions of pounds sterling, which means two hundred millions of francs. He is one of the richest of the peers of England, but there are many richer than he. The Duke of Westminster, for instance, whose fortune is something incredible.

The word nobleman, in English, is almost synonymous with rich man ; this is the secret of the prestige enjoyed by the aristocracy. The day on which the aristocracy have the right to dispose, according to their pleasure, of the property which now increases day by day on account of the law of primogenitureship, they will cease to be a political power, they will become just what their French brethren are, a group of prejudiced men.

The English *parvenu* is still more objectionable

than his like in France, because he has not, as the latter has, a certain leaven of admiration and respect for knowledge and talent. When he is in good society, the Frenchman contents himself with rattling his guineas ; while the other will tell you, without hesitation, that he might have turned his hand to poetry or painting, or easily learnt Latin and Greek, if he had set himself about it ; but that, like a good Briton, he preferred to be useful to his country and go in for business. Barring this, the two types are similar, always excepting this little difference—that the French specimen has invariably arrived in Paris in wooden shoes, and with forty sous in his pocket, whereas this kind of covering for the feet is unknown in England, and the English *parvenu* always comes up to London with only half-a-crown about him.

I happened to be dining one day at the same table as the Lord Mayor of London, the king of English *parvenus.* At dessert, my Lord Mayor brought the subject of education upon the table. The subject was well chosen, for the company was composed of about a hundred journalists, men of letters, and other professional men. " Well, you know," said he, " I admire education very much, but I doubt whether it really does as much good as is supposed ; in fact, I am inclined to believe that it does as much harm as good. According to my ideas, every boy of twelve should be taken from school and put in the way of earning his bread and cheese ; it is quite enough for him to be able to read, write, and cipher, to know a little history and geography. More education than this can only do him harm, by turning

away his attention from the main object of life, which
is to get on in the world.   Look at my case : I left
home at eleven years of age, to learn a trade.   I
never had more than an elementary education, and
yet, you see, I am now Lord Mayor of London."
Such were the remarks, full of good taste, that his
lordship thought fit to make before an assembly composed in a great measure, as I said, of professional
and literary men.

IX.

"HELL is a city much like London," said the great poet Shelley.

London is, indeed, an ignoble mixture of beer and bible, of gin and gospel, of drunkenness and hypo-crisy, of unheard-of squalor and unbridled luxury, of misery and prosperity, of poor, abject, shivering, starving creatures, and people insolent with happi-ness and wealth, whose revenues would appear to us a colossal fortune.

Except at the East End, the poor are not confined to any special quarter of the capital; you may see them everywhere, clothed in rags and degradation. In this free country, the most abject human beings seem to go about clothed with a covering that re-sembles in form the vestures of the upper classes, just to parade their misery in the open street, as a constant reproach to the indifference and contempt of the rich. A celebrated author commits a serious error, an error which only his short stay in England can account for, when he says that there are no beg-gars or low people to be seen in the parks of Lon-don. These places swarm with them, and so do

Regent Street, Oxford Street, and all the great arte-
ries of the town.

Let us take a look at the public promenades.

Hyde Park is a kind of large field badly kept in
order, and situated in the midst of London. There
may be seen by day the richest aristocracy in the
world, on horseback, or in their carriages, going
round and round the gravelled drives. At nightfall,
Hyde Park becomes a resort for cut-throats, a huge
lupanar at sixpence a head, that an Englishman will
advise you to carefully avoid ; the vilest scum of the
streets meet there to wallow in the mire to their
heart's content ; the gates are left open purposely
by night. The policemen who stand at the entrance
could easily cleanse this hotbed of vice ; but they
have express orders not to meddle in that which, it
would appear, is not their business. The London
populace is a malignant one ; it is best not to meddle with it.

By the side of Hyde Park stands Kensington Gardens. This place has something of the solemn gran-
deur of a wood about it—something uncultivated
that delights the eye. It is like a good mile of the
Forest of St. Germain in the heart of town. In
France, our public gardens are placed under the
care of some ex-sergeant, whose ideas never soar
beyond obeying the orders of his superior, and keeping everything in line. If a refractory leaf does but
attract his attention, *une, deusse*, it disappears. Our
trees in the Tuileries look like the little green imi-
tations that are put into children's toy farmyards.
Good old Abbé Gaultier, from whom we have all
learnt a little geography, speaks of the famous park

of Versailles, where Art has forced Nature. Over here, Art leaves Nature alone, because the English respect and appreciate her much more than we. Nothing is more imposing than the exuberant beauty of the English parks. Take a walk across them in the early morning, when there is no one stirring, and the nightingale is singing high up in some gigantic tree ; it is one of the rare pleasures that you will find within your reach in London. If the morning be fine, you will not fail to be struck with a lovely pearl-gray haze, soft and subdued, that I never saw in such perfection as in the London parks. Regent's Park, Green Park, and St. James's Park, the latter especially, which is near to Buckingham Palace, Whitehall, and the Palace of Westminster, are exceedingly fine.

I advise all who pay a visit to London to wander outside the city, and take a look at Kew Gardens, Richmond Park, and the chestnut trees of Hampton Court.

Let us now turn to the streets.

What strikes one at first sight, is the nomenclature of these streets. England, who can boast with reason of the finest literature in the world, does not name her streets after her great literary worthies. When names were wanted, no one thought of Shakespeare, of Spenser, of Gibbon, of Sterne, of Goldsmith, of Burns, of Thackeray, of Dickens, of the hundreds of names that alone would be sufficient to make England glorious for ever. The streets here are called after the aristocracy, the principal towns of the kingdom, and the landlords who built the first houses in them : Bedford Square, Russell Street,

Grosvenor Square, Liverpool Road, etc.   It is true
that I know a Milton Street, and an Addison Road ;
but it must be remembered that Milton was secretary to Oliver Cromwell, and wrote religious poems.
As to Addison, it is not to his poetical works or his
essays that he owes the honour of having a street
named after him ; it is to the fact of his having been
a statesman driving his carriage and pair through
London streets.

The main thoroughfares are now paved with wood.
This kind of paving is very good for the horses and
carriages, also for the contractors, who are constantly
being called into requisition to mend it.

Something that astonishes a Frenchman in London is to see well-dressed men smoking their pipes
in railway carriages, on omnibuses, and even as they
walk in the streets.   I do not say that they are
always perfect gentlemen, but they are men who
look well-bred : business men, bankers' clerks, etc.
The men of the lower classes all appear to me to
smoke new pipes.   I never see any blackened ones.
Peculiar taste !   When they have used a pipe two or
three times they throw it away.

The enormous size of London makes it necessary
for most people to pass from an hour and a half to
two hours a day in an omnibus or train.   This perpetual movement must tell on the brain.   Those
who value their health at all do part of the distance
on foot.   In this country, where the climate is damp,
and the food and drink are the reverse of light, exercise must be taken ; it is the first thing an English
doctor advises you.

On entering one of those little constructions that

we call *vespasiennes*, but which do not at all resemble them, you will see in front of you, "Adjust your dress before leaving." Here, not the slightest move ment must shock modesty. I admire that.

Let us take a walk.

From eight o'clock in the evening, the finest part of London is entirely given up to debauchery. It is a human meat market. I have said elsewhere that respectable Englishmen do not walk about in the evening. The men that you see in Regent Street are mostly foreigners, or provincials who have come up to town for a round of dissipation. Several years ago, the public ball-rooms were closed, and the market, which used to be held within four walls, is now transferred to the open street. The *police des mœurs* does not exist in London, and the capital of this country, so moral and so Christian, exhibits sights too heartrending to imagine. Girls of fourteen or fifteen, with dyed hair, and wan-looking faces daubed with paint, stand about drunk and in rags, soliciting the passers-by for a vile wage. Worn out with fatigue, they drop in the gutter at day-break. They have been up and down the street six mortal hours! It is horrible! The inhabitants of London are beginning to take the matter up : petitions are being prepared. It is high time.

The drunkenness in the streets is indescribable. On Saturday nights it is a general witches' sabbath. The women drink to almost as great an extent as the men. In Scotland, they equal them. In Ireland, they surpass them. My authority is an official report made to the English Government in 1877.

I find the following advertisement in the *Christian*

World: " The wife of a clergyman of the Church of England wishes to recommend to a Christian family, a cook formerly given to drinking, but who has taken a firm resolution of leading a better life." Dear good lady! Why does she not take her herself? Ah! I will tell you why. The worthy lady is not selfish ; clergyman's wife though she be, she does not wish to monopolise all the opportunities of doing good ; she leaves some for you, you should be grateful to her.

The Englishman is only noisy when he is drunk ; then he becomes combative and wicked. One-half the murders one hears of are committed under the influence of drink. It is not so very long since a gentleman was not ashamed to be seen tipsy in the street. At the beginning of the century they went to Parliament in this state ; it was rather good form. There is a story which says that Pitt one day went to the House of Commons leaning upon the arm of an honourable friend. They were both of them drunk. " I say, Pitt," cried the great statesman's friend, " how is it? I can't see the Speaker."

" That's funny! I—shee—two," replied Pitt.

I remember hearing a drunkard one day in Cannon Street station—it was at the time when a war between England and Russia appeared imminent—challenging loudly the latter country. " Come on, Russia, I'll manage you," he shouted. As Russia did not make her appearance : " Well, then, come on, Turkey ; Russia or Turkey, I don't care which it is. The same silence on the part of the Turk. " Well, then, come on, Russia, Turkey, England, I'll fight the b—— lot of you." He was got into a carriage somehow. I pity his poor wife if he reached home without having slaked his thirst for battle upon one of the European Powers.

The saddest spectacle that man, in his degradation, has yet given to the world, is a file of sandwiches. Two boards are slung over the sandwich-man's neck, one on his chest, the other on his back, and he is sent about the streets placarded with the strangest, most grotesque advertisements. For the meagre pay of a few pence, he has, all day long, in all the samples of weather that this cold, damp climate affords, to pace along the gutters of the principal streets. I say *in the gutter*, for he is not allowed to leave it, lest he should intercept the traffic, either of the road or the pavement. I have seen these poor wretches dragging one tired foot after the other, and encased in great square trunks, that covered them from knee to neck. Only their heads and arms were free, and even the arms were not at liberty altogether, for they had to distribute to the passers-by the circulars of a trunk-making firm. Our *chiffonniers* are princes in comparison with these poor beasts of burden :

" Plutot souffrir que mourir
C'est la devise des hommes."

You will not have gone a hundred paces along the street with a valise or bag in your hand, without having a band of street boys and loafers at your heels. They are all on the look out for a chance of earning a penny, if you confide your luggage to them to carry, or of disappearing round the corner with it, if you turn your back an instant. If you require to cross the road, a beggar in rags will step in front of you, and sweep away the mud out of your path with his broom. You will come across these poor devils in the most fashionable quarters : in Piccadilly, in Regent Street, at Hyde Park Corner, under the very windows of Buckingham Palace even.

The most flourishing businesses in London, and the only ones that are really substantial, are those of beer and of old clothes. No credit for the poor man : to get his glass of beer he must come down with his three-halfpence. The publican and the pawnbroker are the princes of English trade. The one is the consequence of the other. Each is the best friend of the other.

In England, the Government does not interfere in these matters ; it does not monopolise any industry, does not undertake to supply the taxpayer with brimstone matches that will not light, and threepenny fireproof cigars.

The needy person applies to the pawnbroker. The manner in which these gentry, whom I have heard magistrates plainly call receivers of stolen goods, carry on business, favours and encourages theft. *Ma tante*, who, in France, corresponds to *my uncle* on this side of the Channel, is obliged by law to pay the person who pledges or sells any object of value in that person's own residence. This, at any rate, is a slight guarantee. Here, you may give the pawnbroker the first name and address that occur to your mind, and he pays you. He lends at the rate of thirty per cent., and advances as little as he can, because he takes all articles at his own risk ; if they have been stolen and are subsequently identified by their rightful owner, he is obliged to restore them.

The language of the streets is beyond everything tnat any French dictionary places at the disposal of the translator : all idea of conveying a notion of it must be renounced. Just as choice, euphemistic, and free from objectional expressions as is the language of the well educated classes, just so crude and obscene is that of the lower orders. These latter seem to have but one adjective at their disposition, the adjective bl——y. This word, which corresponds to our oath *sacré*, makes one shudder in England. To French ears, it can only sound ridiculous. An English workman will say, for instance, " I told my —— master that he only gave me a —— sovereign every —— week, and that I wanted five —— shillings more. He said he had not the —— time to listen to my —— complaints," etc. And so on all the while. This word, however, which happens to be now spelt like the synonym of *sanguinary* is, we believe, no other than a corruption of the expression *by'r lady* (*by our lady*) which we come across several times in Shakespeare.

Cock-fighting and dog-fighting, so famous in former days, are now forbidden by law. Boxers themselves have ceased to be an attraction ; they are liable to prosecution, and only meet for a match clandestinely. These remnants of barbarism are fast disappearing. These combats were terrible. The Englishman hits a blow that would knock your head off your shoulders. This is a curious thing : even

5

when these savages fight in earnest, they never kick each other; it is contrary to the national spirit. The kick is reserved strictly for the weaker sex, who enjoy the whole and sole monopoly of it.

It would be difficult to say where London begins and where it ends. The postal radius extends twelve miles around Charing Cross; which makes, for the circumference of the town, about thirty French leagues.

London has, so to speak, no monuments. The Abbey and Palace of Westminster, St. Paul's,—you must not look for much else. A few statues: the great Cobden, shivering with cold, in a dirty, out-of-the-way corner; Nelson, stuck upon a roman candle, high in the air; three Wellingtons and a Shakespeare; this last a private gift. At the four corners of Trafalgar Square, the London *Place de la Concorde*, four pedestals are to be seen. Three are surmounted by statues, the fourth is waiting. Not that there is any dearth of great men in England: it is simply indifference, nothing more.

The Albert Memorial, a monument erected by the Queen to the memory of Prince Albert, is worth looking at, were it but to show how easy it is to fool away three millions of francs.

The Monument is a column two hundred feet high, erected in commemoration of the Great Fire of London that occurred in 1666. For threepence you can go to the top of it; but, as the keeper says in one of Charles Dickens's novels, "it is worth twice the money not to make the ascent."

John Bull is serious and business-like, he does not waste his powder and shot upon sparrows. Public monuments are frivolous things in his eyes. Yet, what treasures and riches are hidden in such frivolities! Nothing attracts you without, everything enchants you within. London streets are certainly more useful than ornamental. Nothing in them invites you to loiter; on the contrary, everything induces you to push on. There are no strollers in London; in a park they would be thought suspicious characters. Every gentleman you pass in the street is going to his business or on his way home.

The London fog of universal reputation is of two kinds. The most curious, and at the same time the less dangerous, is the black species. It is simply darkness complete and intense at midday. The gas is immediately lighted everywhere, and when this kind of fog remains in the upper atmospheric regions, it does not greatly affect you. It does not touch the earth, and the gas being lighted, it gives you the impression of being in the street at ten o'clock at night. Traffic is not stopped; the bustle of the City goes on as usual.

The most terrible is the yellow fog, that the English call pea-soup. This one gets down your throat and seems to choke you. You have to cover your mouth with a respirator if you do not wish to be choked or seized with an attack of blood-spitting. The gas is useless, you cannot see it even when you are close to the lamp. Traffic is stopped. Sometimes for several hours the town seems dead and buried.

These fogs are not so common as our excellent fellow-countrymen believe. They have an idea that in order to avoid getting lost in London streets, you must not let go your companion's hand, or, at any rate, not wander beyond reach of his coat tails. These fogs scarcely appear more than fifteen days out of the three hundred and sixty-five. During the rest of the year you have always much about the same grayness. When the sky is clear, it is lovely ; but it rarely is clear. When the sun makes his appearance he is photographed, that folks may not forget what he is like. Fogs are beginning to be a little less dreaded ; the Corporation have taken the matter in hand. Several meetings have been held upon the subject. The Lord Mayor has a hand in the pie. Besides, we are told that London is soon to have a new Government. So you see there is hope.

Let us quickly be off and get into the museums, the clubs, the houses ; we shall there find plenty to delight our eyes, minds, and hearts.

X.

If nothing is more sad and gloomy than out-of-
door life in the large English towns, nothing that I
know of is more charming than the interior of a
well-kept English house. It is a paradise of studied
comfort and well-understood luxury.

How sensibly these English people understand
comfort; with what ingenious forethought are the
smallest needs anticipated, what care and study are
expended upon every convenience of life! Sofas
for cosy chats, easy chairs with book-rests, for
reading in; smoking chairs, *ad hoc*, every seat in
the room looks as though it had been invented to
satisfy a special need. Drawing-room, parlour,
library, smoking-room, each has its special use.
Every Englishman has his *boudoir* (I use the word in
its etymological sense), that is to say, his little *sanc-
tum*, whence the vulgar are excluded, and where he
can take refuge when he wishes to work or rest. He
calls this place his growlery, a name having, as you
see, the same meaning as our *boudoir*.

Carpets are things of primary importance in

England. Every floor and staircase, in even the simplest houses, are covered with them. We say in France, that provided an Englishwoman has her carpet and her tea she is happy. These two things are indeed indispensable to her happiness: two primary necessaries of life. I can say from experience that when I am in France, it never enters my mind to ask for tea, but in England I cannot do without it; the climate demands it. "In Scotland," a Scotchman will tell you, "I could not exist without my glass of whiskey;" and he adds, 'but in England, I can do without it," which I am quite ready to believe, although I never saw it.

In a country where winter lasts eight months of the year, where the gray, dull, dirty dampness, that the Englishman is fond of calling *most unusual weather*, fills you with the spleen, it was imperative to seek for happiness at home.

On the outside, the private mansions have nothing remarkable about them; but what wealth and luxury are hidden behind their high dark walls! This, however, is nothing to compare with the great country seats, the ancient homes of Old England; royal domains are they. Picture to yourself a country studded with Chateaux de Fontainebleau.

It is to the country you must go if you would see John Bull in all his glory. Sportsman to the backbone, there he is in his element. "The foreigner who would form a correct opinion of the English character," says Washington Irving, "must not confine his observations to the metropolis. . . . It is in the country that the Englishman gives scope to his natural feelings. He gladly breaks loose from the cold formalities and negative civilities of town, throws off his habits of shy reserve, and becomes joyous and freehearted. He manages to collect round him all the conveniences and elegancies of polite life, and banish its restraints. His country-seat abounds with every requisite, either for studious retirement, tasteful gratification, or rural exercise. Books, paintings, music, horses, dogs, and sporting implements of all kinds are at hand. He puts no constraint, either upon his guests, or himself, but in the true spirit of hospitality, provides the means of enjoyment, and leaves everyone to partake according to his own inclination. . . .

"But what most delights me is the creative talent with which the English decorate the unostentatious abodes of middle life. The rudest habitation, the most unpromising and scanty portion of land in the hands of an Englishman of taste becomes a little paradise. The great charm, however, of English scenery, is the moral feeling that seems to pervade it. It is associated in the mind with ideas of order, of quiet, of sober, well-established principles, of hoary usage and reverend custom. Everything seems to be the growth of ages of regular and peaceful existence."

And the clubs, those Pall Mall palaces! The *Athenæum* Club, for the celebrities of the literary and scientific world ; the *Carlton* for the most important members of the Conservative party ; the *Reform*, for those of the Liberal party ; the *Oxford and Cambridge*, for members of the two great Universities ; the *Army and Navy*, for officers of each service ; I find a list of ninety-nine clubs in Whitaker's Almanack, which omits the names of several unimportant ones. These great clubs are so many princely habitations reserved for the noble and the wealthy : entrance fee, forty pounds ; annual subscription, ten pounds. *This is holding the sugar-plum rather high.* These great clubs are magnificent and very imposing, I admit ; but the lackeys in knee breeches, the sound-killing carpets an inch or two thick, the broad staircases, the immense rooms that seem to be limitless in height, width, and length, the members coming and going without thinking of removing their hats, each ignoring the other or muttering through closed teeth a "How d'you do?" which is equivalent to "Leave me alone, I have no time to talk to you ;" all this freezes me, and I should strongly suspect every one of these luxury-surfeited men of feeling terribly bored, if I had not been thoroughly convinced of it by having seen them yawning behind their *Times* fit to put their jaw bones out of joint.

The only club that does not strike me with a respect akin to awe, is the *Savage* Club. This somewhat Bohemian fraternity is composed of literary men, writers, artists, and actors. The Prince of Wales was brave enough to be made a *Savage* last year, and has taken his after-dinner smoke in the club like the humblest of his brother Savages. The varied talents of the members form a special attraction of the dinners and other meetings of this interesting association. The entrance fee is eight pounds, and the annual subscription three.

A volume would scarce suffice to convey a correct idea of the treasures contained in the museums of London : the British Museum, the South Kensington Museum, the National Gallery, Hampton Court Palace, the Tower of London, and I know not how many more.

BRITISH MUSEUM.—Reading-room in rotunda form, with glass cupola, undoubtedly the finest in the world. In the middle of the room are librarians, intelligent, obliging, and noiseless ; in circles are arranged commodious tables, comfortable chairs, every requisite for reading and study, including tranquillity ; around you 600,000 volumes. The printed book section contained, in 1882, more than 1,300,000 volumes. Catalogues perfect. In Paris, to find a book, you must know the name of the author and the date of the first edition. A friend of mine lately wrote to me from Paris to ask me for a list of all the French works that treat of Shakespeare. In one hour, at the British Museum, I obtained a complete list. Galleries of pictures ; architecture ; Egyptian, Assyrian, Greek, and Roman antiquities—among which may be seen the Mausoleum, one of the seven wonders of the ancient world ; Cleopatra's coffin ; the Ilgi seal (date 2050 B.C.) ; the marbles of the Parthenon ; the bas-reliefs of Phidias and from the Temple of Ægina ; columns from the Temple of Diana at Ephesus ; the epitaph of the Athenians killed at Potidœa. These treasures were bought from Lord Elgin, who obtained them in exchange for a clock that may still be seen in the Bazaar at Athens. Then there are bas-reliefs from the Temple of Apollo, carved tablets from Nineveh and Babylon, etc. I repeat, it would be idle to attempt to enumerate here all these priceless treasures. Marvellous natural history collections, comprising part

of the skeleton of a fossil man. Collections of manu-
scripts, coins, engravings. A botanical museum, a
geological museum. A room with Etruscan vases,
etc., etc. The British Museum is open to the public
on every day, except Sunday of course, so that one
never meets with workmen or others of the lower
class. At the Louvre, you see more workmen than
well-dressed people. "A coin two thousand years
old !" I once overheard a worthy peasant fellow exclaim ; "that's a good joke ! We're only in 1868
now !"

SOUTH KENSINGTON MUSEUM.—Schools of Art and
Science ; splendid library of about 50,000 volumes ;
collections of pictures by English masters ; museum
of antiquities ; Handel's harpsichord ; an organ that
belonged to Martin Luther ; a collection of *objets
d'art* of the Middle Ages and the Renaissance. The
Museum contains 617 oil paintings, and 1,291 water-
colours. The Indian section is most interesting : Indian temples, Vedic and Puranic gods ; illustrations
of the whole of the Hindoo mythology.

NATIONAL GALLERY, founded in 1824, with the
magnificent collection of Mr. John Julius Angerstein.
This collection, as its name implies, is almost entire-
ly composed of the works of the great English
masters : Hogarth, Reynolds, Gainsborough, Wright,
Lawrence, Turner, Leslie, Edwin Landseer. You
may also see there pictures by Raphael, Rubens,
Rembrandt, Poussin, Correggio, Leonardo da Vinci,
Titian, Van Dyck, Murillo, Velasquez, Salvator
Rosa, etc.

THE TOWER OF LONDON.—On the banks of the
Thames, in the midst of the City, surrounded by a

moat, stands this ancient fortress. Built by William the Conqueror, and partly, tradition says, by
Julius Cæsar, it is to this day perfectly intact. Here
are kept the crown jewels, a collection of fire-arms
and the finest armour, the axe and block used at the
execution of Lady Jane Grey, the nine days' queen,
and a thousand other precious historical relics. All
these warders in fifteenth century costumes, these
corridors, these portcullises and moats, carry you
back in thought hundreds of years while you spend
two or three delightful hours in this unique old
place. Just opposite the Tower of London is the
Tower Sub-way, an iron tube, seven feet in diameter,
forming a footpath through the bed of the Thames,
between Great Tower Hill and Vine Street. Mr.
Charles Dickens advises none but the very briefest
of Her Majesty's lieges to attempt the passage in
high-heeled boots or with a hat to which he attaches
any particular value.

HAMPTON COURT.—On the Thames, a few miles
distant from London, stands this splendid palace,
built by Cardinal Wolsey, who presented it to Henry
VIII. It was by a strange irony of fate the favourite
residence of Charles I. and of Cromwell. The park
and gardens are fairy-like. The chestnut trees of
Hampton Court have a world-wide fame ; they are
titanic. The palace contains a gallery of 933 pictures, mostly historical portraits ; also sumptuous
apartments and most beautiful tapestry. Overlook-
ing a lovely landscape that should be seen when the
chestnut trees are in bloom, is a terrace nearly a
mile long. One of the curiosities of this place is a
colossal vine planted in 1769, which bears as many

as 2,500 bunches, each more than a pound in weight.
The trunk which, at its base, measures thirty inches
in circumference, is 110 feet long, and throws out its
branches over a surface of 1,200 square feet. The
exquisitely flavoured grapes are reserved for the
royal tables. The park of Hampton Court is open
on Sundays : well done, John !

WESTMINSTER ABBEY. — Otherwise, Cathedral of
the West, to distinguish it from St. Paul's, which
was formerly called *Eastminster*, or Cathedral of the
East ; the most famous monument in England after
the Tower of London ; built by Edward the Con-
fessor, on the spot where Sebart, king of the East
Saxons, had built a church in 616. Of the first
edifice there remains hardly anything more than the
cloister, which the boys of Westminster School now
use as a gymnasium ; the building, as it stands at
present, is, with few exceptions, the work of the
architects of Henry VII. For more than 800 years
the kings and queens of England have been crowned
in Westminster Abbey. It would be impossible
here to give a description of the tombs, the
statues and busts, the monuments erected to the
memory of all the celebrities who were the pride of
the ages in which they lived. Suffice it to say that,
besides the sovereigns who repose beneath the
stones of this ancient edifice, you are also treading
on the remains of Spenser, Milton, Dryden (*Poet's
Corner*), Handel, Sheridan, Macaulay, Charles Dickens, Thackeray, Livingstone and Garrick, the great
comedian, who certainly is not out of place in the
midst of all these glorious sons of Albion. Above
the tomb of the valiant Henry V. is still to be seen

the saddle and helmet used by him at the memorable battle of Agincourt. The tombstones are in admirable preservation. The best preachers in the kingdom are to be heard at the three Sunday services.

St. Paul's Cathedral.—Situated on the summit of Ludgate Hill, this imposing edifice may be seen from many miles round. This monument of gigantic proportions shares with Westminster Abbey the honor of rendering homage to the great men of a loving and grateful country. St. Paul's Cathedral, such as we now see it, was begun by Sir Christopher Wren in 1673, and finished in 1710, the old edifice having been completely destroyed by the Great Fire in 1666. Here lie the mortal remains of Wellington, Samuel Johnson, Wren, Turner, Joshua Reynolds, and Edwin Landseer. The dome is 404 feet high. It is the most prominent edifice of the English capital.

Crystal Palace.—This immense glass cage cost £1,500,000 to build. The work was no doubt a difficult one, and, to parody the witty saying of Samuel Johnson, it is to be regretted that it was not found to be impossible ; it is but a great ugly toy. The terrace is fine, and the surrounding gardens magnificent. This place is a favourite resort of Bank-holiday keepers, of whom it sometimes attracts as many as a hundred thousand. There are fireworks, choirs of five thousand voices, flower shows, acrobats, circuses, menageries, out-door games of all kinds, the whole for the modest sum of one shilling. The Crystal Palace has a good picture-gallery, a splendid reading-room, a library, a school of Literature, Art and Science. It also boasts a zoological garden.

which, however, is very insignificant when compared
with the magnificent one in Regent's Park, as also
is our own Jardin des Plantes.   As to the collection
of fishes, I advise visitors to renounce all idea of
trying to find any in the aquarium ; but the excellent restaurant of the Palace supplies them, with
their proper sauces, at decidedly moderate charges.

MADAME TUSSAUD'S EXHIBITION.—Capital wax figures of the kings and queens of England, and most
of the important personages of the world.   A museum of historical relics, containing among other
things the knife of the guillotine used during the
Reign of Terror, the principal key of the Bastile, the
carriage used by Napoleon I. in his campaigns, the
shirt worn by Henry IV. when he was stabbed by
Ravaillac, etc., etc.   For sixpence extra you may
make your flesh creep in the Chamber of Horrors,
which contains the portrait models of all the greatest criminals, Marat expiring in his bath, and draw-
ings representing the tortures inflicted upon criminals in different countries.   This exhibition was
established in London, I regret to have to say, by a
Frenchwoman.

XI.

ANIMALS are very well treated in England, even by the roughs of the lower classes in London. The principal reason of this is, that the Society for the Prevention of Cruelty to Animals has numerous agents, and any one convicted of ill-treating an animal is liable to six months' hard labour. Besides, by maltreating a horse you may maim it, and thereby diminish its value. When the London carmen treat their wives as well as they treat their horses, I shall appreciate their sentiments of humanity; as it is, they only remind me of the love of the Turk for his dog. If, in the streets of Constantinople, you were seen to harm a dog, you would immediately have the populace at your heels; but you might serve a woman or child as badly as you pleased, and no one would think of interfering with you.

A few years ago, the Prince of Wales made a voyage to India. On his way, he paid a visit to the King of Spain who, to do honour to his guest, ordered a bull fight to be got up for his amusement. The English did not like it, and began to make a stir.

The Prince of Wales, in fact, is president of the Society for the protection of animals. Like a good Englishman, he abstained from attending the performance.

A Society for the protection of women has yet to be formed. I extract the two following police court reports from the newspapers, where you may see similar ones every day :—

THAMES POLICE COURT.—John H. is charged with having beaten his wife, and threatened to kill her. On Friday night he returned home drunk, seized his wife by the hair, and threw her out of the window. He then sent his five children to join her in the street, whether by the window or not, the report does not state. The woman managed to get into the house again, but the man, seizing a knife, threatened *to settle her*. She succeeded in escaping, but not before he had injured her so brutally about the head, that blood flowed in profusion from her nose and mouth. John H. is condemned to one month's imprisonment. If he had done as much to a horse, he would have got six months at least. But a woman! his *wife*, especially !

In Manchester, and all parts of Lancashire, the men wear iron soled shoes with pointed toes. With these, kicking can be very successfully performed.

Here is the second case. The prisoner is condemned to six months' hard labour. The magistrate is more severe, because the victim is not the legitimate wife of the savage, who would in such case have been able to plead extenuating circumstances.

WOOLWICH POLICE COURT.—William A. is charged with having struck Mary Ann G. The woman appears in court with her head bandaged, and her face covered with bruises. The accused has been beating her for days, and has struck her in the street, in her own house, and in a neighbour's house. It is in the latter place that he beat his victim, with the iron heel of a boot. A policeman states that he found the woman lying unconscious upon the floor in a pool of blood, and adds that the room looked like a slaughter-house. The magistrate remarks that there exists an odious class of beings, who live upon un-fortunate women, and treat them worse than slave traders and corsairs treat their human merchandise. He sentences the prisoner to six months' hard labour, and regrets that the law does not allow him to order him to be flogged every day in his cell.

I read in to-day's newspaper (30th December, 1882) :—"BARROW-IN-FURNESS.—A woman, named Sarah P., died yesterday from the effects of blows dealt her about the head by her husband. Two days ago, it appears, P. had a quarrel with his wife, whom he seized by the hair, and in this manner dragged upstairs to the bedroom. There he knocked her down, and by means of a large hammer literally re-duced her head to a jelly. He then put her on the bed, and slept the night by her side. The accused, who does not deny the charge, is sent to take his trial at the Court of Assizes." You may read such cases *every day* in your newspaper. What are the people taught? you will ask. Certainly it is not religious and moral lessons that are wanting in this country of churches and chapels, of Sunday-schools and Bible classes, of Christian associations, Salvation Armies, and what not! Neither can drunkenness

6

alone entirely account for the savage brutality of these men of the lower classes in England. The cause must be looked for in the law, which does not protect the women.

I find, in the *Daily News* of the 14th November, 1882, the following reflections upon the subject of a sentence delivered the day before. "Our laws relating to assassination and acts of violence, lead to most disastrous consequences. A husband was yesterday convicted of having kicked his wife to death. The jury, not considering that these kicks had been inflicted with the intention of causing death, only found the prisoner guilty of manslaughter, and the sentence passed by the judge was but fifteen months' imprisonment. Such mild punishments are not calculated to diminish the number of cases of brutality towards wives ; on the contrary, they will tend to make certain classes of our society believe that a wife is a kind of property, a sort of domestic animal, that the husband may maltreat at his pleasure, and almost with impunity."

The married woman occupies but a secondary place in society. In low life, the husband stakes her for ten shillings, for half-a-crown, for a glass of beer.

I remember one day a man going to the police-court to claim his wife. The woman contended that her husband had sold her to a friend for ten shillings, that she was quite happy with her new owner, and that on no consideration would she return to her husband, who was in the habit of beating her and keeping her without food.

These savages have also several other favourite

pastimes. When they are not occupied in kicking
their wives in the most sensitive parts of their
bodies, they fight among themselves, and bite off
each other's noses. The olfactory organ would
seem to be a dainty to their taste. I counted, during the year 1882, in the London newspapers alone,
twenty-eight cases of this kind.

The hospitals, like the great public schools and
universities, are each independent institutions, having their own governing bodies and revenues. The
Government has nothing to do with them. Every
one here is master in his own house. From the administrative point of view, England is a confedera-
tion of small republics : *respublicæ in republica.* In
France, charitable institutions spend over a fourth
part of their income in staffs of servants, printers'
bills, and red tape. In England, the governing body
of a hospital is composed of rich philanthropists,
who, instead of charging the poor for looking after
their interest, pay for the honour of doing good.

Each hospital has its school of medicine. This is
a source of revenue. The students pay for their
course of study, and the examinations are made by
the leading men of the Royal College of Physicians
and the Royal College of Surgeons. The prelimi-
nary examination, which admits a student to a hospital, is an insignificant one. This is a mistake, for
numbers of young men waste their time for years in
the hospitals, and are at length obliged, as a last
resource, to go to Scotland or America, and take
diplomas which may there be had without difficulty
England is full of dunces of this kind. Before ac-

cepting them as students, it would be a good plan to make sure that they possessed a certain amount of intellect and knowledge.

The workhouses, the unions, the board schools, in each parish, are supported at the expense of the ratepayers. In the poorer districts the poor-tax amounts to one third of the rent; in the rich ones, there is hardly any poor-tax at all. It is easy to see at a glance that the laws here are made by the land-lords and the aristocracy. It is true that landed property is more valuable in the districts where the poor-tax is lower. Nevertheless, it is hoped that London will soon have a municipal government which will extend over the whole capital, and that the rates will be uniform in all parts of it. The Corporation of London at present only represents the City proper.

The worshipful city companies, to the number of eighty and more, do not now concern themselves much about the various branches of trade that they are still supposed to represent. The mercers, the grocers, the haberdashers, the bakers, the carpenters, etc., are simply noblemen and the princes of finance and commerce, gentlemen who go in for charity on a large scale, with money which does not come out of their own pockets, make prodigious dinners, get their own children and those of their friends edu-cated for nothing, and take part in the Lord Mayor's show every year on the ninth of November. The riches of these companies, which have been accumu-lating for centuries, are beginning to attract the at-tention of the public, who wish to find out whether by better employing this money, which was intended to do good to the needy, the poor-tax might not be lightened. The worshipful companies naturally cry out against such sacrilegious interference ; but, if the municipality of London is ever extended over the whole town, they will be forced to show their cash boxes and give an account of the uses to which they put their colossal fortunes.

The streets are infested with beggars, to whom the English do not trouble to reply, " I have no small change," and of match sellers, bareheaded and barefooted, merely covered with one coating of filth and vermin, and another of rags. If these creatures washed, they would die of cold.

German bands, hand organs, and concertinas are the delight of the poorer neighbourhoods. There exists in London quite a colony of Italians, with dirty yellow faces and bangles in their ears, who live by the hand organs. They are all accompanied by girls in national costume. The greater part of these are English girls whom these blackguards of the lowest stamp have tampered with in more than one respect, and who prefer the adventurous life of the streets to the slavery of a factory life. Organ grinders make, on an average, about ten shillings a day, it appears. It is, as I have said, in streets inhabited by workpeople that they reap their bronze-harvest. They play polkas, waltzes, and especially jigs, and all the inhabitants come out of their slums and dance around the instrument.

The attraction of every popular holiday in England is a band of Christy minstrels, street singers, who rub soot about their faces, get themselves up in extraordinary garments made of great multi-

coloured plaids, and sing vulgar songs, whilst they
accompany themselves upon banjos improvised out
of an old sauce or frying pan. These artists, of
American importation, sing in chorus, dance, grimace,
and see themselves inundated with pennies that fall
from all quarters into their grotesque headgear.

The angel of charity, the lady bountiful! This
is a title to which every woman who has no duties to
keep her at home aspires. The misunderstood
woman—the old maid—that article so common in
England, is the benefactress of the human race. See
her trot along the streets, going to distribute coal
tickets, bread tickets, words of consolation, verses of
the Bible, at the bedside of the sick. Do not stop
her on her way ; she is so busy she has not a moment
to spare ; some one is waiting for her. Go, dear
kind soul, unclaimed blessing, the wretch who dis-
dains your treasures of love will never know what
he has lost !

By hundreds may be counted the charitable associations, the benevolent societies, the hospitals and
workhouses ; and to think that every year is spent,
in Bibles and alcoholic liquors alone, more than
£60,000,000, that is to say, a sum of money which
would not only be sufficient to abolish pauperism,
but which would allow every freeborn Briton to live
like a gentleman.

One of the favourite pastimes of John Bull, the
protector of animals, is pigeon shooting. He does
not always content himself with shooting at the un-
fortunate little bird ; he sometimes puts out one of

its eyes, that it may only fly in a certain direction, and that he may shoot it more easily. This kind of sport, however, begins to be a little less popular, thanks to the charming Princess of Wales, who formally intimated to the public the interest she felt in these poor little innocent birds. Not long ago, the men of the lowest classes used to find great pleasure in flaying cats alive.

Magnanimity, in politics especially, is a virtue of which John Bull claims the sole monopoly. Read his books and papers, and see how he is always offering himself incense until it is a wonder he does not choke. A moralist of the highest order, defender of the rights of small nations, apostle of the suppression of slavery, propagator of the true faith, John does not allow any one else to have a hand in the protection of petty states; it is his privilege and his only. I have not yet forgotten what a state he was in when the French troops entered Tunis ; what a perfect fever of indignation ! What a shower of insults he poured out on our heads! What a drenching he gave us! His transports of fury and abhorrence were epic. As his heart relieved itself of bitterness, it refilled with joy. What ! can it really be you, friend John, preaching to us on the respect due to small nations? You who, for the past ten years that I have been watching you, have made war upon the Ashantees, the Afghans, the Basutos, the Boers, the Zulus, the Abyssinians, the Egyptians, and Heaven knows whom besides. You, who barked at Russia, but did not dare to bite, because you no longer, as in 1854, had France at your side to do the work ! And, even for this little noise, do I not remember that you made the poor Sultan, automaton of all the Turkeys, hand you over the island of Cyprus ? What, John ! has it not also come to my ears that you get a revenue of five millions of francs by enforcing the opium trade *vi et armis?* You know very well where the shoe pinches ; you do not like to have your nose rubbed in your foreign policy—it annoys you, O great philanthropist ! At least, then, be a little charitable, O great and magnanimous Christian !

XII.

CHRISTMAS is the great family *fête* day in England. Rich or poor, every one dines at Christmas. Even the poorest carry, the day before, a miserable little bundle of rags to the pawnbroker, in order to obtain the wherewith to buy a dinner of meat and pudding. Familiar faces are gathered around every fireside. Only at this time of the year does the Englishman lay aside all business cares, and give free scope to feelings of gaiety. On Christmas Eve, Father Christmas, with his long frost-spangled beard, comes down the chimney to fill the stockings that are hung at the bedside, with sweetmeats and toys, just as in France *Petit Noël* comes and fills the little shoes that are laid in the fireplace. Here New Year's Day is not kept as a holiday. Christmas-boxes take the place of New Year's gifts.

The humblest home is decorated with holly and ivy ; the poorest housewife prepares her goose and plum-pudding. The English excel in the art of decorating the interior of their houses. The Christmas decorations are sometimes quite artistic, even the simplest give the house a holiday look ; you see

at once that the day is no ordinary one. Only the
poor postman has a hard time of it ; he must carry
compliments of the season and good wishes to every
door. "To you and yours we wish a Merry Christmas and a Happy New Year," this is the formula.
The poor modern Mercury takes heart as he remem-
bers that after he has delivered compliments of the
season, presents and Christmas-boxes to all, he himself will not be forgotten when the time comes for
him to knock at the door and ask for his Christmas-
box. No one forgets him. I know of no more
universally popular personage than this humble
official. Bearer of love letters, post-office orders,
cheques, little carefully tied packages, all the more
charming that it is difficult to get at their contents,
it is who shall be the first to open the door to him.
He is welcomed everywhere ; smiling faces greet
him at every door. In England, the postman is the
hero of Christmas-time ; so he strikes the iron while
it is hot, and on Boxing Day comes round to ask
for a reward which all are ready to give without
grudging.

The mistletoe plays an important part at Christmas. Besides all the ivy and holly with which look-
ing-glasses and pictures are framed, branches of
mistletoe are suspended from the ceiling. This part
of the decorating is superintended by the young girls
of the family, who have their reasons for making
sure that the mistletoe is conveniently placed, for
every young fellow who surprises a girl beneath it
has a right to put his arm round her waist and give
her a kiss.

The king of the day, however, is indisputably the

plum-pudding. You should see faces light up with pleasure, and little mouths stretch out on the entry of the majestic monarch, crowned with holly, and exhaling a perfume which brings joy to every heart. I must say that I never properly appreciated the plum-pudding, but I have always accepted a slice. To refuse a helping of this dainty would be to cast a chill over the family feast, to play the sorry part of a kill-joy : you might as well refuse the bread and salt of Russian hospitality. The English seem to be the only people who appreciate these cakes and puddings, of which the little Corinthian grape is the chief ingredient. It is Greece that supplies these little black berries. "If France, Russia, and America," says M. About in *La Grèce Contemporaine*, "were possessed with the same craving, the consumption of this product would be unlimited, and Greece would have in her vines an inexhaustible source of revenue."

It is no small matter to make a plum-pudding. Judge for yourself, here is the recipe : Take a pound and a half of raisins, stone them and cut them in halves, and add half a pound of currants. Chop a pound of suet and a pound of orange and lemon peel, and mix with ten ounces of grated bread-crumbs, a pound of flour, a spoonful of baking powder, ten ounces of sugar, half a pound of almonds, eight eggs, salt, spices, half a pint of pale ale, and a quartern of brandy. Mix well and boil for eight hours. If you do not find your pudding tasty enough to please you, I advise you, next time, to add a decoction of half-an-ounce of shag. This will give it a finishing touch. The quantity of beer brandy, and spice, that a lower class cook puts into her pudding, renders it a perfect ball of fire ; you are obliged to grasp the table, and hold on tight, whilst you swallow a mouthful or two of it.

Most of the theatres give a pantomime at Christmas. These pantomimes, as they are wrongly called here, are absurd cock-and-bull stories, founded upon the Arabian Nights or the fairy tales, and gorgeously put on the stage. In the performance of Robinson Crusoe, for instance, you see a procession of all the kings and queens of England, from William the Conqueror to Queen Victoria, a Lord Mayor's Show, and a review of English troops at Cairo. People enjoy that, and find no fault with it. No wit about these productions. Dazzling costumes, splendid ballets, and pretty girls by hundreds. When the curtain has fallen after the transformation scene, the performance terminates with a harlequinade in which the poor policeman—Bobby, as he is called— comes in for all the blows and never succeeds in collaring the clown who has run off with the leg of mutton. The laughs are all at the expense of poor Bobby. I have always failed to understand the innocence, or appreciate the morality, of the English harlequinade.

Sunday, in England, being a day of funereal gloom, and not a holiday, it was thought necessary to give the people a few days of rest or rather of pleasure. Sir John Lubbock passed a bill in Parliament, a few years ago, by which the banks were enjoined to close on four days in the year : Boxing·

day, Easter-Monday, Whit-Monday, and the first
Monday in August. These are called Bank-holidays.
The English people, keepers of Saint Monday *par
excellence*, have seized the occasion by the forelock ;
all the shops follow the example of the banks ; the
manufactories and workshops give up their workmen and workwomen ; the slums and sinks of London vomit their unclean contents. The days on
which these popular saturnalia are held, you must
stay at home and draw your blinds.

These lower classes in England form a curious
subject for study. They alone preserve the tradi-
tions of Old Merry England. Regardless of the
future, living from hand to mouth, bohemian to
the backbone, noisy and coarse, they form a most
striking contrast to the rest of this nation of ants,
morose, frigid, and still preserving the same dread
of happiness and joy as in the days of John Knox.

It is the same difference as that which existed,
in the eleventh century, between the Saxons and the
Normans, when, on the eve of the battle of Hast-
ings, which laid England at the feet of William the
Conqueror, the Normans spent the night in prayer
and the Saxons in riotous drunkenness.

At eight or nine in the morning, the public-
houses are ready, the animals are let out of leash,
the riot begins. The sky-blue, apple-green, blood-
red figures appear, shouting and dancing to the
strains of concertinas ; the penny cigars are lighted,
the mob is in motion. The *fête* opens with drink,
continues with drink, and closes with drink ; it is
the whole day one desperate struggle between the
container and the contained, in which the latter is

often worsted, and evacuates the field. Few or no
games. They knock down cocoa-nuts with short,
thick sticks, play pitch-and-toss, or mount the
merry-go-rounds; nothing else. No plays : the
English lower classes never go to a theatre. The
people crowd into the open spaces to drink, dance
and lie about. The more furious fight, and wind
up the fun of this national holiday by a visit to the
lock-up. For days the streets are full of stragglers ;
it is a whole week lost, drowned in beer. Such is
the result of the philanthropic measure of Sir John
Lubbock. The police are indulgent on these
days : if every drunkard had to be immured, the
prisons would have to be enlarged. They only lock
up the most froward—those who reply with their
fists to the policeman's recommendation to go
home. I remember one day seeing from my window a policeman take into custody a young woman
of about eighteen, dead drunk. She was trying to
bite and kick the poor constable. The mother was
behind, vociferating imprecations. "Ah ! you rascal !
Why can't you leave her alone? Poor dear ! She
ain't done nothink : she's drunk, that s all."

I notice, in the newspapers of the 27th of
December, 1882, under the title of *Holiday Charges*,
a list of charges for drunkenness the day before.

Here are the figures :—

Bow Street Police Court	.	.	33
Westminster	"	. .	45
Clerkenwell	"	. .	43
Worship Street	"	. .	52
Marylebone	"	. .	70
Lambeth	"	. .	104

(of whom 57 were women.)

Southwark Police Court		.	.	27
Greenwich	"	.	.	48
Hammersmith	"	.	.	26
West Ham	"	.	.	36
Hampstead	"	.	.	62
Highgate	"	.	.	30
Woolwich	"	.	.	56

This list does not contain the names of all the police-courts, and, I repeat it, only the most furious are incarcerated on Bank-holidays.

XIII.

THE cookery of John Bull leaves much to be desired. In this country—it was Voltaire who said it—there are fifty different religions, but only one sauce. Do not fancy, however, that John does not like nice things. When he is in Paris, can't he ferret out the good corners, that's all! But then that is quite another matter. In Paris he has no need to make a parade of goodness, while in London he is obliged to. In England, he goes to church; in Paris, he goes to Mabille. Of course it is perfectly understood that it is only to look on, and to be able to describe to his wife when he returns home how wicked those dreadful Frenchmen are.

In the aristocratic households, and in the principal clubs, French cooks are kept, and the table is excellent.

In an ordinary middle-class family, the Sunday dinner consists of a large joint of about ten pounds weight, and excellent in quality, I must say, for English meat is superior to any. It is accompanied by boiled potatoes and other vegetables. A few families of free-thinking tendencies with regard to matters of routine, commence the repast with a *potage au poivre;* but they are not yet very numerous. This Sunday joint is partaken of cold on Mondays, and in the form of a pudding on Tuesdays, with the same vegetables. Vegetables, as a separate course, have yet to be known. Asparagus, young green peas even, are plainly boiled and eaten with the meat, and badly boiled, as a rule ; they have to be crunched rather than eaten. Asparagus with white sauce or in salad, spinach or peas *au sucre,* even fried potatoes, that democratic dish, all such things would be considered epicurean. Here Puritanism is carried even as far as to the kitchen. It would seem that man had been placed in this world to deny himself the good things that the Creator put in it.

In Scotland, things are still worse. Walter Scott relates that, when a child, he one day took the liberty of exclaiming before his father : " Oh ! how nice the soup is !" The Puritan parent forthwith ordered a pint of cold water to be added to it.

The head of the family says grace before and after the repast. In low-church or dissenting families, the father repeats grace for one or two minutes. He does this to remind you that you are not at table to enjoy yourself, and you soon find out that he is right. Everyone is motionless and silent. If you venture a remark, you receive monosyllabic replies. You are asked if you will take a little more beef, and you reply : " No, thank you," or "If you please, but only a very small piece." Of these two alternatives you had better choose the first, it is the more proper. If you are

7

asked, as you certainly will be, "Have you been long in England?" and "How do you like it?" be sure and say exactly how long you have been over, and that you like England very much. Do not venture into details, that would be a conversation, and nobody would be grateful to you for breaking the solemn silence. After you have been thus seated at table about an hour, you will be seized with a longing to shriek, or to pinch your neighbour, to ascertain whether he is alive or only pretending. You had better mind, or you would not get invited again, which you would regret very much.

If John dines frugally at home, it is in public that you should see him at table. His appetite and his epicurism are then revealed to an astonishing extent. The public dinner is an eminently English institution.

The king of banquets is the one given by the Lord Mayor, on the ninth of November, the day of his installation at the Guildhall.

All the City companies, all the clubs, and all the societies hold their annual banquets. One of the finest London dinners, the most interesting perhaps, is that given by the Royal Academy of Painting. Politics are excluded. It is the rendezvous of all the aristocracy of Nature in England. Cabinet ministers, eminent members of the House of Lords and of the House of Commons, conservatives or liberals, bishops, generals, judges, scientific and literary men, artists, lawyers—every great man of the day is to be seen at that table. The Prince of Wales and his brothers never fail to honour this banquet with their presence.

These dinners cost fabulous sums of money—from five to eight pounds a head. The turtle soup, which invariably heads the *menu*, costs a guinea a quart. The rest to match.

At dessert, the loving-cup is passed around, and toasts and speeches begin. The English, who have been used in the debating societies of the public schools and universities, to speaking in public, excel in after-dinner speeches, which are sometimes perfect little masterpieces of *àpropos* and humour.

First come the patriotic toasts : the Queen, the Prince of Wales, and the other members of the Royal Family ; the army and navy, the Houses of Parliament. Then comes the toast of the evening, that is to say, that the success of the club or the society is drunk, or the health of the principal guest, if the dinner is given in honour of some hero of the day.

Ladies are seldom invited to these banquets. When they are included, however, the assembly breaks up after the toast to the ladies.

These dinners last from four to five hours.

When you go to a party, the servant, before showing you to the drawing-room, conducts you to the dining-room, and there asks you whether you take tea or coffee. You promptly reply that you take tea. The coffee is generally atrocious, simply because no one knows how to make it, or will take the trouble of making it properly.

Tea, which is still in France a luxury, costing twelve or fifteen francs a pound, is excellent in Eng-

land for two francs and a half. So the poorest families can indulge in a cup of tea night and morning.
It is the favourite drink of women, and the cure for
all ills. "Ah! sir," said an old Norman peasant-
woman to me one day, "my coffee—after the sweet
Jesus—is my salvation!" Tea plays the same part
over here.

The tea-kettle is, like the *pot-au-feu* in France, the
emblem of domestic virtue.

It is when John drinks his tea very hot in tiny
sips, nibbling a bit of bread-and-butter or of toast,
that he is really beautiful and edifying. Nearly all
the middle-class take tea at five o'clock, and still
make a meal of it. Better still : John sometimes
gives what he calls a tea-party, a compound noun
which I would not attempt to translate into French.
Then, besides bread-and-butter and toast, the table
is laid out with preserves, and black dry cakes, very
much like gingerbread in colour and taste. The
old maids are in the seventh heaven. You should
see them, forcing angelic smiles over tusks an inch
long, with their eyes chastely cast down, and their
hands folded on the edge of the table, waiting for the
lady of the house to ask them if they take milk and
sugar, or if their tea is sweet enough.

"Is your tea as you like it ?"

"Oh ! very nice, thank you."

The body remains motionless, bolt upright, the
head alone turns slightly.

"Will you not take a little cake ? "

"No, thank you, only a tiny piece of bread-and-
butter."

At dinner, if conversation flags at every moment,

beef and pale ale are there to keep you alive at any
rate, but with these slops and slices, you have not
even strength enough to attempt to enliven it. You
give up the idea at the outset, and it dies in agonies.
Shelley has described these

> "   .   .   .   .   teas
> Where small talk dies in agonies."

It is appalling.

> "   .   .   A party in a parlour,
> .   .   .   Some sipping tea,
> But as you by their faces see,
> All silent, and all —— damned."

We must, however, do justice to English hospitality. You will never be invited to a party, be it
ever so modest, without being asked to sit down to
a good supper. When somebody proposed to us,
young men in Paris, to take us to a ball, we never
failed to inquire beforehand whether there was a
supper to be expected. Needless to ask such a
question in England : *cela va sans dire.*

In France, to this very day, and in very good
houses indeed, the mistress of the house will ask you,
about one o'clock in the morning, whether you would
like to take a cup of chocolate !

No, we shall never be serious like the English.

XIV.

THE English, with their free institutions, do not give their magistrates the power of judging them. In all cases, criminal or civil, it is a jury who finds a true bill against the prisoner, decides upon his culpability or innocence,* returns a verdict for plaintiff or defendant, and fixes the amount of damages. The judge simply interprets the law, and pronounces judgment. If, in his summing up, which should be a clear and impartial statement of the evidence for and against the prisoner, he allows his personal opinion to transpire, you should see how the papers of the following day are down upon him and take him to task. The prisoner becomes the object of universal sympathy, and an explosion of public opinion seldom fails to immediately obtain for him a mitigation or compensation. We all remember the Staunton case : the four prisoners were condemned to death ; but, a few days after, three of them had their sentences commuted to penal servi-

---

* And there is no condemnation unless the jury all agree upon their verdict. If they do not, they are discharged, and the case is carried before another jury.

tude, and the fourth was set at liberty without delay.

In France, we give almost unlimited arbitrary
powers to a legion of badly-paid* magistrates, who
are for the most part—in the provinces at least—the
failures of our Bar. I warrant that there are more
judges in a French town of 50,000 inhabitants than
in the whole of England.

There are few countries in which democratic tendencies are more marked than in France. In spite
of this, public opinion does not concern itself about
judicial proceedings, because there is no country in
which authority is less respected, although, strange
to say, there is not one in which it is more feared
and more easily submitted to. We seem to accept
all forms of tyranny in order to shirk all responsibility. Democracy with us chiefly consists in holding up to ridicule a despotism, the acts of which we
in turn approve by holding up to ridicule those who
are the victims of it. Upon the least suspicion, a
magistrate may order, on his own responsibility—a
responsibility, I may add, which no one has a right
to question—he may order, I say, a search or an arrest in any private house.

Personal security is differently understood by
other free nations; the United States for instance.
Here are two articles from the Statute Book of that
country :—

"The right which every citizen has to enjoy the
security of his person, his abode, his papers, and
effects, against unreasonable searches and seizures,

* About £70 a year.

shall be inviolable ; no warrant shall be issued except upon well-founded presumption, corroborated
upon oath."

" No person shall be called upon to answer an
accusation unless a true bill has been found against
that person by a grand jury."

In England, a man who is arrested and informed
of the charge brought against him, says : " You will
have to prove it ; " and the inspector at the police
station tells him : " I must caution you against making any statement. In fact, anything you may say
will be used in evidence against you."

If, in France, a man is accused of stealing a watch,
the *juge d'instruction* invariably says to him : " The
best thing you can do is to make a full confession ; "
or, " You are charged with stealing a watch, prove
that you are innocent." In England, the accused
person is told : " You are charged with stealing a
watch, you have nothing to say, we shall have to
prove it." Such are the two different manners of
proceeding. No inquisition in the shape of private
examination. No *prévention*—that is to say, that,
except in grave cases, the prisoner is liberated on
bail. He appears before a magistrate, in public, the
very day after his arrest. If he makes a full confession, the magistrate advises him to reserve his defence and to plead not guilty. He is not made to
undergo any examination, and it is preferred that he
should not admit his guilt, in order that, by independent evidence, the charge may be brought home
to him. Besides, it is quite common here to see
people giving themselves up to justice, and as-
serting that they have committed some crime. It is

a very frequent mania. When any case of murder remains obscured in mystery, all the drunkards take it into their heads that they committed it, and they go and give themselves up to the police. An inquiry is made, and they are set at liberty.

The examination of the witnesses is done by counsel. The judge presides over the proceedings : he acts as moderator. The prisoner is quietly seated in the dock : he listens ; the poor witnesses pass an uncomfortable quarter of an hour in the hands of the lawyers.

In order that the jury may not be influenced by the antecedents of the prisoner, if they should be bad, no reference to them is permitted.* If he is found guilty, a member of the police comes forward to prove that the prisoner has already undergone several sentences, and then the judge applies the full rigour of the law. As to the witnesses, every effort is made to show that their evidence is not trustworthy. The most incongruous questions are put to them. Woe betide them, if there exist any page in their past life that they would fain keep secret! "Are you married to the man you live with ?" a woman may be asked. "Are you a faithful wife ? Is it not a fact that you are addicted to drinking ?" She has to answer all this. There are some who get angry over it, and the audience enjoy the fun.

English judges are chosen from among the shining lights of the bar ; they receive enormous emoluments and are irremovable, two conditions quite in-

---

* See Appendix (A).

dispensable to their independence. John Bull pays
his servants well, but he expects to be well served.

The era of liberty began with the French Revolution nearly a hundred years ago. Since that time,
Heaven knows how many governments and con-
stitutions—all *immutable* and *perpetual* of course—
France has had. A curious fact, however, well
worth noticing, when we consider the progress of
that liberty bought at the price of so many bloody
revolutions, is the survival of Article 75 of the Constitution of the Year VIII., after three monarchies,
two empires, and two republics.

This article, as every one knows, runs thus: "Government officials, with the exception of ministers,
can only be prosecuted for offences having reference
to the discharge of their duties, by virtue of a
special decision of the Council of State, and the
case shall be heard in an ordinary court of justice."

Article 75 of the Constitution of the Year VIII.
owes its existence to the most tyrannical spirit of
the century : it was suggested to Siéyès by the First-
Consul at the time when the latter was quietly pre-
paring to entomb the liberties of the country.

The monarchies that succeeded the first empire
took good care to preserve an article so invaluable
to despotism. Before the Revolution, the Government covered the acts of its agents by illegality and
absolutism ; since the Revolution, it has covered
them by the law. It is an improvement.

Thus a Government official can only be prosecuted by virtue of a decision of the Council of State.
Would not such an appeal be a perfect farce ? Does

not the Council of State emanate from the Executive Power ? Is it not part and parcel of it ?

In England, you collar a policeman who has insulted or touched you, and give him in charge. The following day, you appear against him, and if you can prove your case he is condemned ; and yet, although his little staff constitutes his whole equipment, he is more respected than our *sergent-de-ville* with all the war materials that he carries about. It was not long ago that I saw him with a sword and a revolver.

The following incident occurred in England not long ago. Two mounted policemen, who had arrested a man, were proceeding to a police-station with him ; but as he refused to follow, one of them alighted from his horse and attached him to the saddle. The unfortunate fellow, not being able to keep up with the horse, fell and was dragged along the road about a length of fifteen yards. The spectators, indignant, stopped the two policemen, and gave them in charge. They were tried and condemned to seven years' penal servitude.

The English have a love of pettifogging : it is in the Norman blood. This peculiar taste is an expensive one, especially in England, where, though justice is prompt and decisive in criminal matters, it is slow and costly in civil ones. A barrister of the least reputation will not put on his wig for less than £20. A Queen's counsel demands fabulous fees. The solicitor, the general lawyer, does the work of our *notaires*, *avoués* and *huissiers ;* he can even plead in the police-courts. His bills of costs are master-pieces in their way. Here is one :—

		s.	d.
1.	To receiving a letter from you, and reading it	3	6
2.	To writing the answer	3	6
3.	To hiring a cab	5	0
4.	To thinking of your affair in the cab	3	6
5.	To listening to your remarks	3	6
6.	To answering them	3	6
7.	To meeting your father-in-law and speaking to him of your affair	3	6

One wonders how much a solicitor would charge his client for dreaming of his affair. And so the *seeings*, *beings*, *goings*, *thinkings*, &c., at three-and-six a piece, cover dozens of pages.

Judges and barristers still wear the powdered wigs with pig-tails of a hundred years ago. " *Tel rit d'un juge en habit court qui tremble au seul aspect d'un procureur en robe. La forme, la a forme !* " says Brid'oison, who is not dead yet.

The English love their old monuments, their ancient castles, their time-honoured customs. We French people are Vandals. You can, at the present time, see the Tower of London, exactly as it stood hundreds of years ago ; and the people, who visit its dungeons, can see for themselves the progress that man has made. In France, no more *Bastille*, no more *Donjon de Vincennes* to be seen ! The very names of our streets die with each government. What a mistake ! I believe that, if every town in France had a Waterloo Place and a Sedan Street,

the remembrance of the empire would remain en-
graved on their hearts for a long time to come.

John Bull executes more criminals than all the
other European States put together.* Extenuating
circumstances are not taken into consideration in
trials for murder. It is sufficient, in England, to be
convicted of having wilfully taken the life of a person to forfeit one's life. The law makes no distinction between one who has committed murder in a
moment of passion or jealousy, and one who has
long premeditated the death of his victim to satisfy
the basest of cravings.

"During my visit to the United States," says M.
Alexis de Tocqueville, "I saw the inhabitants of a
country, in which a great crime had been committed, spontaneously form committees for the
purpose of bringing the criminal to justice." This
is all very well, but the occupation of amateur de-
tective is an ugly one. A criminal may, it is true,
be an enemy of mankind ; still, one cannot help feeling pleased to know that there are men who, for a
consideration, will willingly track, arrest, condemn,
and hang him. In England, when the perpetrator
of a crime cannot be found, the police have the walls
of a town covered with placards, offering a reward
of 100, 200, 500 pounds sterling, according to the
gravity of the crime, to whoever will give such in-
formation as shall lead to the apprehension and
conviction of the criminal. The plan often succeeds,
especially in Ireland, among the Fenians. An ac-

---

* See Appendix B.

complice often obtains his own pardon by denounc-
ing his confederates ; the approver has always played
an important part in the history of crime in Ireland.

Hanging gives instantaneous death, and causes no
suffering, say the English.   This may be ; but the
rope often breaks, and I have known Marwood to
bungle over his work more than once.   He has had
practice enough ; he ought to know the ropes by
this time.

A propos of hanging :

Whilst the Shah of Persia was on a visit to England, he wanted to see how the English executed
their criminals.   The sight of torture is a favourite
entertainment of Eastern monarchs.   Accompanied
by a numerous suite, he went to Newgate, the London *Roquette*.   Great was his disappointment upon
hearing that the rope gave instantaneous death.
However, he decided upon seeing how the apparatus
worked, and desired the governor of the prison to
be good enough to execute a criminal on the spot.
It was represented to him that there were no
criminals lying under sentence of death just then.
He was about to lose his temper, when, recollecting
himself, he cried, " That's no objection ; I will let
you have one of my suite. "

The London folks have not forgotten it yet.

XV.

Duels—A sensible Duel—Polygamy—A good, charitable, Christian Polygamist—Different ways of looking at a question—Blackmail levied in parks and streets—The Thief's Eldorado.

In England, a duellist who had killed his adversary would be tried for murder; if he had wounded him only, he would be tried for attempt to murder. The Englishman regards that man as eminently ridiculous who, after being insulted, asks for six inches of cold steel through the body as compensation. In the lower classes, an insulted man pays his insulter cash in the form of one of those blows such as John Bull alone knows how to administer. The men of the better classes carry their complaint to the law-courts and get damages awarded them. There is sense in that. As I write, a sculptor has just been condemned to pay a brother sculptor £5,000 for having said of him in a newspaper that he was not the author of all the works that he had given to the world as his own. Our great duellists would only be pitiful heroes at the Central Criminal Court here in England.

There is nothing like a good fine of a few thousands of francs to strip a man of that halo of chivalry and romance that a sword in the hand surrounds him with. The duel is treated seriously in France, where, for that very reason, it is not likely to die out just directly.

For my part, this is how I understand duelling: " Sir," wrote a German journalist to a Russian one a short time ago, "your article upon German women is infamous. I deeply regret that the distance which separates us prevents my boxing your ears as you deserve, but I beg you to take the will for the deed, and to consider yourself well and duly cuffed, by your humble and obedient servant."—The Russian replied by return of post : "Sir, just at the time when you were cuffing me, the happy idea of drawing a revolver from my pocket and blowing your brains out on the spot occurred to me : I therefore beg you to consider yourself as quite dead and duly buried. Your very humble and obedient servant."

The polygamist, who is punished in France with from five to ten years' penal servitude, gets off with a few months' imprisonment in England ; indeed he is oftenest acquitted. In this country, where desertion is so frequent in married life, where marriage is so easy, and the *registre de l'Etat civil* is unknown, the accused persons can always, with good chance of success, plead the departure of the spouse, and ignorance of his or her existence. People set out for Canada, Australia, or New Zealand, maybe get wrecked ; or if they ever arrive in port, do not give any more account of themselves. Such cases are happening daily. In France, with our administrative organisation, a debtor or bankrupt has no chance of escape ; in England, you would more easily catch a sparrow by the tail.

Moreover laws and customs in England encourage marriage. Concubinage is rare, except among the lower classes; the formalities of marriage are so elementary that it is really not worth while to dispense with them; and so, instead of taking a mistress, a man marries. An Englishman may marry his wife's sister without binding himself to anything. He takes her to church, presents her to the clergyman as Miss So-and-so, and is married to her. The marriage is illegal, and he may marry again as he chooses.

I extract the following lines from an account of the cross-examination of a witness by the counsel for the defence.

"A witness," cries Pierre Chopart in the *Courier de Lyon*, "cheer up, old fellow! Witness! That's respectable, at any rate!" In England, the position of a witness is no enviable one, I can assure you. Whether you be on the side of plaintiff or defendant, you will have to submit to a cross-examination at the hands of the counsel of the adverse side, and you will pass an uncomfortable quarter of an hour. See what you think of the following :—

Counsel.—"You have had more experience of women than the accused, I believe."

Witness.—"No."

Counsel.—"You got married in 1875, did you not?"

Witness.—"I decline to answer that question."

Counsel.—"But you must answer it."

Witness.—"Well, then, I think I did."

Counsel.—"You married Miss Mary Jane E——, did you not?"

8

Witness.—" I did."

Counsel.—" Is she still alive ? "

Witness.—" No, she is dead ; (recollecting himself) I should say, that is to say . . . . well, yes, she is still alive."

Counsel.—" Did you marry in 1879 ? "

Witness.—" I did."

Counsel—" Was the lady's name Miss E. A—— ? "

Witness.—" My second wife was my first wife's sister ; the marriage was illegal."

Counsel.—" That makes three, does it not ? How old are you ? "

Witness.—" Thirty-two."

Counsel.—" When did your first wife die ? "

Witness.—" In 1876."

Counsel.—" Nevertheless, you married her sister in 1875 ? "

Witness.—" I did."

Counsel.—" Are these the only women you have married ? "

Witness.—" Yes."

Counsel.—" Are you quite sure ? "

Witness.—" Perfectly sure."

Counsel.—" You tell us that you think the accused guilty. How came you to treat him as a friend up to the moment of his arrest ? "

Witness.—" I do not see why one should cease to treat a man as a friend because he has committed a fault. I would be friendly with a man who had committed the greatest crime in the world if by so doing I could help him in any way."

Counsel.—" What ! even if he had married his wife's sister, and abandoned her afterwards ? "

Witness.—" Certainly."

Counsel.—" You are an excellent Christian, I see. Now tell us . . . ." &c.

I extract the following lines from the newspapers :

HAMMERSMITH POLICE COURT (2nd March, 1883).—A soldier is accused of bigamy. The first witness is a policeman who states that on the way to the police-station the accused said to him, " I did not know I had been married a second time. I had been drunk for a fortnight, and I did not have the banns published. It was only yesterday I found out that I had got married again last Thursday."

The Magistrate to the Prisoner.—" What have you to say ? "

Prisoner.—" Your worship, I have separated from my wife, to whom I allow one and ninepence a week by order of my colonel : I am living with another woman. The other day, this woman threatened to throw all my clothes out in the street if I did not marry her. Then we had something to drink together, and it seems we went to church and got married."

I read in a case of the same kind the following statement (*Exeter Western News*):—

The Judge to Witness.—" How is it you were not ashamed to go to the altar with a drunken man ? "

Witness.—" Well ! my lord, if he hadn't been drunk, he wouldn't have gone."

I know a worthy Englishman who, not long ago, married a fourth wife, of whom he is the third husband ; he is but sixty years old, and may fairly hope to make up his half dozen.

There are very few old bachelors in England. All

the men marry : some for love, some for money, and some from a sense of duty.   It is a debt they owe to society.   It is not that they are fond of women, for, like Solomon, they generally abuse them.   Women will never forgive the magnificent Hebrew monarch for having spoken ill of their sex, after having married seven hundred of them, and even added to that number three hundred concubines.   Men, on the contrary, consider that, having had so much experience, he ought to be the best authority on the subject.

A woman alone is safer in the streets of London than an unprotected male.   A woman risks having her purse stolen ; a man risks more : he risks his reputation.   He may be stopped by a woman who will say to him in an indignant tone : "Give me five shillings, or I will call a policeman.   You have insulted me !"   Or, it may be, a young girl, often a little girl, who will come up to you and politely ask you to tell her the time.   Without suspecting harm, you take out your watch and you are immediately surrounded by several individuals who rob you, or accuse you of having insulted the girl.   Dreading a scandal, you pay rather than be dragged into an unpleasant affair.   There exist thousands of people who live by this kind of highway robbery ; who are always on the watch for persons whose respectable appearance seems to mark them as easy victims of such infernal machinations.   I know few men in London to whom this kind of adventure has not happened once at least.   The parks and the Thames Embankment especially are places that every man who values his honour should carefully avoid, even in broad daylight. Never sit down alone out of doors; never speak to a child of the lower class; and, if ever you should fall into a trap of the kind, pay on the spot; do not hesitate an instant, for the police will not help you and the Police Court magistrates, who are the failures of the English Bar, will simply say to you : " I am quite willing to believe that you are not guilty, but what did you go into a park for ?" This is a literal quotation , I heard it myself.

The Englishman does not stroll about. When his business is finished, he goes home at a brisk pace, and never walks out in the evening. At nightfall, the parks and unfrequented places are entirely given up to thieves and prostitutes, and the police take no notice of it. There still exist in London large neighbourhoods into which it would be dangerous to venture even at mid-day, unless you were accompanied by detectives. These are curious sights to be seen in John Bull's capital, and the Scotland Yard authorities will always obligingly provide you with two or three guides, if you care to visit them.

If, in this ants' nest of nearly five millions of souls, Scotland Yard took it into its head to stamp out the dens of robbers, the number of policemen would have to be more than doubled. It is preferred to trust to the good sense, wisdom, and economical principles of respectable people, who already find the taxes quite heavy enough, and prefer to avoid risking themselves in the parks and other public resorts set aside as hunting ground for pickpockets and street prostitutes.

XVI.

THE English are fond of laughing at the great number of people wearing orders that are to be met with in France. It is a fact that their name is *legion*. The red ribbon is to be seen occasionally in London, but it is not in the least appreciated : those who know what it means smile, the rest take this bawble for an ornament of some kind or a peculiar whim. The Frenchmen, living in England, who have decorations, do not wear them. There exists however no law to forbid their being worn ; in fact, in England, you might cover your breast with stars and ribbons, dress yourself as a Polish General, a Swiss Admiral, or in the shortest of kilts, no one would think of following you as a guy. You may make yourself ridiculous if you like, but you will have no law to fear but the law of common sense, no judge to dread but public opinion.

The subjects of Her Britannic Majesty can only accept foreign orders by permission of the Queen, and, with the exception of soldiers in uniform, no one wears them in the street. As to English orders, they are scarcely ever conferred upon any one outside the aristocracy, the army and the diplomatic circle. Civil servants, learned men, writers, and artists scarcely ever get them ; and, with the exception of a few sovereigns who are Knights of the Most Noble Order of the Garter, there are very few foreigners who possess English decorations.

When I say that there are no decorations to be seen in England, I am wrong. More than six hundred thousand people, men and women, now wear a blue ribbon in their buttonhole. Some are drunkards, who have pledged themselves to abstain from all alcoholic liquors, and others are good young men who have solemnly promised never to drink anything intoxicating. These people form the Blue Ribbon Army. In England, it is desirable to be virtuous, if you can ; but whether you are or not, it is indispensable to appear so, and young Englishmen of the middle class, young clerks and shopboys, even the urchins of the National Schools, are happy to have an occasion to stick a certificate of virtue in their buttonholes. Advertisements such as the following are to be seen in the papers every day: "A young clerk wanted ; a good Christian and a member of the Blue Ribbon Army preferred." So the number of blue ribbons increases every day. I read the following lines in one of the principal newspapers: "A new league against drunkenness is now being formed in London. The members pledge themselves to drink no alcoholic liquors except at meals. Their distinctive badge will be a yellow ribbon." If these set themselves up for heroes, I should like to know what airs the blue ribbon folks will be giving themselves. Whatever comes of it, good luck to the yellow ribbon !

England is a martial but not a military nation. Her army is not very popular at home, and for very good reasons. The officers are gentlemen and well-educated men, but the private soldiers do not represent the English people in the least. The ranks are composed of fine-looking fellows who have enlisted in order to lead an easy life, and wear a scarlet uniform that will make them the darlings of the sex who will look at no other man while they are near.

The love of John Bull for his soldiers is somewhat curious. He gives them ovations, showers decorations on their heads when they return home after rounding off his estate ; but, if he goes to a public place of entertainment, and meets a soldier there, away he hurries, exclaiming : " This place is not respectable : soldiers are admitted." In the singular the warrior loses all his prestige. So he who admires hair in the mass on the head of a lovely woman, would make a wry face if he happened upon *one* in his soup, even though it had strayed from the tresses of this beloved one.

Uniforms, so popular in France, are scarcely known in England. Prefects, mayors, engineers, civil servants, government clerks, drivers, conductors, undertakers even, all have their uniform. Here, unless you go to soldiers' barracks or to a review, you will always see officers in private dress. Only non-commissioned officers and private soldiers go about in uniform, and even they are forbidden to carry arms. The drivers and conductors of omnibuses wear ordinary hats and coats. The workman wears neither blouse nor cap, the uniform of our *prolétaires* in town and country. The form of dress is the same in all classes ; it is only from the degree of dirtiness of an Englishman's coat that you can judge to which class he belongs.

The most flourishing business in the poorer neighbourhoods is that of the dealer in second-hand clothes. The rich wear their clothes for a week or two, then give them to their servants, who wear or sell them. After these coats, hats, and shoes have changed hands from six to ten times, you will see them upon the lower working-classes, who wear them until they fall to pieces. If I were not afraid of parodying *Figaro*, I might say that these people never quit their clothes—it is the clothes that quit them.

Then the beggars pick them up, and cover their bodies with them as best they can. Some of those befeathered hats might inspire a lyric poet with a modern Odyssey. It is a spirit of independence and equality which, badly understood, makes the poor copy the rich in their dress. It is likewise a feeling of pride—well understood, I think—which makes the working-classes of France prefer plain, but new, clothes.

With the exception of the boys of Christ's Hospital, who still wear the same costume as the students in Edward VI.'s time (yellow stockings and dark blue cassock), English schoolboys have no uniform, except for athletic games, when it becomes necessary for them in the lists to be distinguished from the opponents to whom they have sent a challenge.

Besides the regular army, the reserves, and the

militia, Her Majesty could rely in time of need
upon the services of 400,000 Volunteers. These
warriors—very inoffensive, I may venture to say—
are for the most part young city men and bankers'
clerks, happy to have an opportunity of leaving
their desks two or three times a year to go and
breathe some fresh country air. They can never
be called upon to serve outside the territory of the
British Isles ; and as, in England, sunstrokes are
not to be feared, they are all pretty sure to end
their existence comfortably in their beds. The Life
Insurance companies have in their prospectuses a
paragraph concerning them which I think a little
bit sarcastic :—"The premium of insurance is fixed at
so much. This premium does not apply to military
men, sailors, or any person whose occupation places
his or her life in danger. *Volunteers pay the ordinary.
premium.*"

XVII.

THE English do not speak foreign languages flu-
ently : but the fault lies with themselves.

Their dignity is the object of their constant care.
Ever fearful of compromising it, they will not place
themselves at a disadvantage by speaking a foreign
language, when there is chance to speak their own.
I know a great many Englishmen who speak
French exceedingly well, but who infinitely prefer
speaking English, even with French people, who
murder their language. They have an idea that
a man is always more or less ridiculous when he
is speaking a language not his own . . . . and
they naturally prefer that that man should be *you*.

It is useless to tell them: "Go on ; do not be
afraid. What can it matter to you that people
should discover your nationality, when you speak
French ? You are English, and you are right to
be proud of it; why fear to let it be seen?" A
celebrated man has said: "Never place your
confidence in an Englishman who speaks French
without an accent." This celebrated man is no less
a person than Prince Von Bismarck.

On the other hand, an Englishman knows very

well that go where he will, he is sure to find a
Hôtel d'Angleterre or an *Hôtel de Londres*, and, if
his purse will allow of it, he will take care not
to put up at any other. If he has to work for his
living, he knows that the English language will be
quite sufficient for him, in England or in the
colonies. For that matter this is a sentiment shared
by his neighbours across the Channel. In every
country that is capable of providing for its children,
you see a certain amount of indifference regarding
the study of foreign languages. It is not so in
Germany, and some other countries, where a
knowledge of French and English is necessary to
those who would earn their living. I do not speak
of Switzerland, which has two maternal languages.
It is difficult to persuade an Englishman that it is
something more than a mere accomplishment that
he is acquiring when he studies a foreign language.
It must be admitted, too, that he has natural difficulties to contend with. French vowels are bold
and well marked; English ones are uncertain. The
Englishman never lays stress enough upon our
tonics; he will always pronounce our word *plaisir*
more or less like *plaisiar*. In school, he is not taught
to speak French; he is made to translate *Télé-
maque*, the works of Rollin and Barthélemy, or
those famous selections of *Contes à dormir debout*,
such as have almost driven mad generations of professors and pupils in French schools. He is likewise
made to read the *Roman de la Rose*, nay, even the
Chanson de Roland; but if you asked an English
schoolboy to give you the French for "How do
you do?" you would greatly puzzle him.

Almost all the young girls speak French passably when they leave their schools, where resident French governesses speak their language to them all day long. Besides, in the Englishwoman, as in the woman of every known country of the globe, the hypoglossis is more pliant than in man ; it is a more powerful and better perfected mechanism. Man will never be able to compete with woman in the study of tongues.

I once remarked to the head-master of a large school, speaking of one of his pupils : " You have a boy there that ought to speak French very well, if he will but take the trouble : his pronunciation is capital." "Oh ! I do not doubt it," he replied ; " he is full of affectation."

In France, we call every man *monsieur*, no matter what his nationality may be. Not so the Englishman ; he does not apply his word *mister* to strangers ; he believes he does honour to the French, the Germans, and the Italians, by giving them the titles of *monsieur*, *herr*, *signor*. In an account of a concert you will read such paragraphs as the following : "The trio was admirably played by Herr Joachim, Signor Piatti, and Monsieur d'Almaine."

Monsieur is a word that the English invariably pronounce very badly, in spite of constant efforts, for which they deserve credit. In England, you will always hear yourself called *mossoo*, *mossiay*, *mochoo*, *mochiay*, or *mounzier*, and you should take it as a compliment, because it is really intended as such by John : *monsieur* is but a corruption of *monseigneur* ; so, you see, it is almost as if he called you *my lord*.

The English language is constantly getting enriched with French words. Ought I really to say
enriched? It seems to me that, on the contrary, a
language is impoverished by borrowing, not words
alone, but whole phrases from a foreign one.

Neologism has invaded literature, journalism, and
conversation. In certain novels this craze is carried
to a ridiculous point. In the last century, after the
victories of Blenheim and Malplaquet, Addison lifted
his voice against this irruption of French words, and
asked that the law should interdict the use of them.
Purists begin to be once more alarmed.

In France, during the past century, it is true we
have borrowed some words applying to political
economy, sport, manufacture, and navigation especially ; but they are only words, and words of
which the greater number had previously been borrowed of us by our neighbours, such as *budget, tun-
nel, jockey, jury, fashion,* &c., that the English had
themselves made out of *bougette, tonnel (tonneau), jac-
quet, juré, façon,* &c.

The English language of the present day borrows
entire phrases from our own : *à outrance, par excellence, hors de combat,* and hundreds of others.

French fashions have quite taken root over here,
and have brought a vocabulary of their own with
them. Besides, Englishwomen, who are much more
easily shocked by the name of a thing than by the
thing itself, have been very happy in avoiding the
English names of certain more or less unmentiona-
ble parts of their dress. The words *chemise, corset,
corsage, veste, tournure,* &c., are all English words now.
Indispensable pieces of bed-room furniture are all

called by their French names. These foreign words
just suit the euphemistic character of the English
language, which always expresses less than it leaves
to be guessed ; which employs undecided words,
and always beats about the bush.

A French schoolboy who has not prepared his
lessons, will say to his master : " I have not done
my lessons, sir." To appease the master's wrath,
he may shed one or two crocodile's tears ; the young
English schoolboy will employ circumlocution.
" Please, sir, I am afraid I have not learnt my lesson," or, "I don't think I have learnt my lesson ;"
he is seldom very sure. If he is quite certain, and
has a valid excuse, he has more assurance. " Please,
sir," said a little fellow to a professor of my acquaintance one day, "I have not prepared my translation ;
Grandmamma died last night." "Well, I suppose
you must be excused this time, but tell your grand-
mother not to let it happen again," replied the master. Another time an exercise full of barbarisms
and solecisms was presented. "The work you have
brought me this morning is shameful," said my
friend. "It isn't my fault, sir ; papa always *will*
help me," pleaded the pupil.

One of the most eminent professors of French in
England told me one day that there is a certain
class of students incapable of learning our language.
They are the sneaks, the tartufes, the children of
puritan people, who at home never speak above a
whisper. Our language, so frank and outspoken in
tone as well as expression, sticks in their throats,
and will not pass those teeth that are never unclosed,
or those lips that open with difficulty : undecided,

vague, sticky phrases suit them best : phrases such
as only the English language admits.   "When I am
going to examine a class," he said to me, "I run my
eyes along over the pupils' faces and discover at a
glance those that will give me good answers—those
who will reply in French if ' ask them ; they have
good open faces that do not shun your gaze.   Those
that look askance, squinting and looking ill at ease,
you will get no French out of, take it for granted."

The English language is composed of about 43,-
000 words, of which 29,000 are of Latin origin and
14,000 of Teutonic extraction.   The greater part of
the Latin ones passed into the English language
through the Norman dialect.   This being so, the
French language ought to be easier for the English
than for the Germans ; yet the latter speak it much
better than they.

An impetus should be given to the improvement
of the teaching of French in England.   The two
most free and intelligent nations in the world, already united by so many links of race and language,
ought to understand and study each other better.
It may fairly be hoped that these two nations, who
already respect each other, will, at no distant future,
change that respect into a love to be shaken by no
calumny, by no earthly power.

XVIII.

The French Colony—French Societies.

THERE are about thirty thousand French people established in England, and the number is increasing every day.

Twenty years ago—not more—our compatriots living in this great city knew little or nothing of one another.

It was sufficient to announce yourself as French to have the door of the French Embassy closed in your face.

Every man is more or less wary in a foreign land. When he is on the Continent, the Englishman shuns his compatriots; at least he does not seek their acquaintance. "Who are they at home?" he says to himself.

This feeling no longer exists in London among the French colony, now large, industrious, compact, and united.

Besides the French Benevolent Society, the French Hospital, and several associations of more or less importance, in 1880 there was founded in London a French National Society, reckoning at the present time nearly a thousand members.

I extract the following from its statutes :—

" The growing importance of the French colony

9

in London, the large interests represented by it, have created the desire for an organisation capable of uniting its various elements and binding them together into a compact whole, and of keeping alive among its members the exalted sentiments of patriotism and humanity.

" I. A society for the benefit of the French residing in England has been formed and denominated the 'Société Nationale Française.'

"II. Its special aim is to create relations of esteem and friendship among its members by giving them facilities for becoming known to each other ; and its general aim is to defend the interest of the colony and to study philosophical and moral questions.

"III. In order to facilitate intercourse between those members whose tastes or occupations are similar, three sections have been formed :—

" 1. A commercial section for the study of commercial questions.

" 2. A scientific and literary section for the study of the progress of science and literature.

" 3. An artistic section concerning itself with the fine arts, and able to give a special attraction to the general meetings of the society by the help of the talent which some of its members may possess."

This society is destined to render very great service. What cannot be done individually can be done collectively.

Material interests will not be the only ones protected by this association. The French National Society will keep alive in the hearts of all its members the love and remembrance of the mother-country, too soon forgotten in this land where every one lives for himself and to himself. The French National Society gives frequent entertainments, sometimes a ball, at other times a concert or a dramatic performance. These social gatherings make those who join in them forget that they are in exile, an exile none the less sad for being voluntary. They are in France once more in the spirit.

Let us hope, however, that they will not be too exclusive, but that they will continue to study our good neighbours, the English. Many French people in England carry their horror of everything English to a ridiculous extent. I know one who has lived nearly twenty years in this country, but who boasts of not knowing a word of English. I know others who, on the contrary, delight in disparaging our dear country whenever they have an occasion ; who have altered their names to make them appear more English, and whose only regret is that they have not red whiskers.

Both courses are equally to be avoided.

The mission of the French who live in England is a double one : it should be theirs to make France known to the English, who, with the exception of some who travel, know it not ; they have also to make us better acquainted with England, hitherto a closed letter for us.

Now, listen well : I will tell you what the Standard Geographies teach English boys and girls about us.

FRANCE (*Character*).—" In France, the tradesmen leave the management of their business to their wives, while they themselves are at *cafés*, promenades, or other places of amusement. . . ." " Licentiousness is a prominent characteristic of the nation.

Every third mother is unmarried, and every third child has a stain on his birth." *

Upon the principle that everything which is printed must be true, children swallow all these incongruities like so much gospel ; it is with such materials that their heads are stuffed. This is the result : I extracted the following from the essay of a National School child, which an examiner had the indiscretion to show me. I keep the style intact · " English trade is honest, but French is far from being so. . . . The depredations committed every night on our coasts by French corsairs compel us to keep, at a great expense, a whole army of coastguards."

We are not much farther advanced in France. A compatriot, to whom I had spoken of a young English aristocrat who was going to settle in Australia, wrote to me one day : " What? he is going to settle in Australia! Can it be possible? Going to live with savages ! "

M. Blanchard de Farges, French Consul-General in London, in a very clever speech that he made at the Congress of French teachers, held in the month of January, 1883, expressed himself in these terms :

* This quotation, I will admit, must have taken away the breath of many an English reader of my book. I think, however, that two English papers, including the *Daily News*, might as well have taken it for granted that I was giving a faithful quotation, instead of insinuating that it was more or less a fabrication of my brain. The first part of the quotation is to be found in Cornwall's Geography, and the second in Mackay's. These books have run through over a hundred editions, and are in use everywhere. I feel convinced that, in exposing such vile teaching, I shall have every fair and right-minded Englishman on my side.—MAX O'RELL.

"Gentlemen, I will not allow myself to be drawn into the subject of politics, which would be out of place here, and which are neither to my taste, nor exactly within my province ; but I will say, or, rather, I will repeat, without quitting my own department, that if we knew all our European neighbours as well as we are known to them, we should spare ourselves many disappointments, or, at least, many a false step. It is a fact of which I receive ample proof every day, and, if it will not be trespassing upon your time, I will, with your permission, explain my meaning.

"Gentlemen, every French mail brings me dozens of business letters. These letters sometimes drive me to despair, because, though I have every desire to give satisfaction to their authors, they themselves put it out of my power to do so by calling upon me to perform impossibilities, which prove on the part of most of them an utter ignorance of England, her institutions, and customs. Some ask me to use my private authority, and take vigorous proceedings against a defaulting debtor or a swindler ; others call upon me to restore a missing wife, husband, daughter or son, just as if I had a brigade of policemen at hand to collar them, and put them on board the French boat by force, without any more ado. The greater number set me the task of finding out, in this great maze that we live in, a certain person whose name they are kind enough to give me. In this way, a provincial town councillor appealed to me a short while ago, to inform him what had become of a certain Miss Gordon of the United-Kingdom, whom he had had the extreme pleasure of meeting at the seaside. In the same manner, a worthy family lately asked me to give them some news of a missing member who, said they, "had enlisted in my army, and was serving in the colonies *n c-irlandaises.*"

The French National Society has given rise to another Society no less useful ; I mean the National Society of French teachers in England. The professors of French language and literature in the Universities and great Public Schools are men of high attainments; but outside these great institutions are to be found numbers of talented teachers, who, through not occupying positions that bring them into notice, have the mortification of seeing themselves confounded with hundreds of impostors of all nations, not excepting France, who call themselves teachers of French.

A clever young professor in London had the happy and patriotic idea of grouping together all the French teachers really worthy of the name, and of forming an association having for aim, firstly, to develop and improve the teaching of French, and to spread a knowledge of the language in England : and secondly, to establish a fund for providing aged and infirm members with pecuniary assistance and pensions. Our great Victor Hugo is Honorary President of this young Society, and the names of our *savants* and most illustrious literary men are to be found on the list of its Honorary Committee. An English Honorary Committee is in process of formation, and everything seems to promise a brilliant future for this interesting association.

Although all the needs of the French colony would appear at first sight to be satisfied, there is still another which makes itself felt : it is the want of a French *lycée*.   Our compatriots in London are obliged to send their children to English schools.   Many of them have married English women, and the hybrid issue of these marriages is all but lost to France, and even incapable for the most part of speaking French.   Parents begin to feel concerned about this state of things, and think that a *lycée*, combining the advantages of a French education and English training, would respond to a need which is felt more and more every day.

In short, confidence is restored, patriotism has shaken off its lethargy, and the French Colony in England, which increases every year in number and importance, will ere long be a little power capable of playing a part of the first order, to the profit of both France and England.

XIX.

THE theatre of England has fallen during the nineteenth century as low as it was possible for it to fall.
How is this to be accounted for in a country that
has produced a Shakespeare, and which boasts such
a galaxy of good poets and novelists ?

The fault lies a little with the audience, who, if
they are judges of dramatic art, do not show it in
public. It would be bad form to applaud in a theatre, and worse still to hiss. I have heard actors
sing horribly out of tune without a murmur being
raised by the audience. John Bull pities the poor
artiste who endeavours to amuse him, but fails in
his efforts ; and, being of a magnanimous turn of
mind, he forgives him.

He does not identify himself with the action of the
play : he does not forget that it is but a play. The
actor who sings with taste, and throws himself with
passion into his part, appears to him supremely
ridiculous. He regards him as a poor mountebank
who has to earn a living and

" . . . pour le servir, abjuré son cœur d'homme."

In Italy, I have known an audience correct a tenor, and give him the right note when he sang flat.

The English lower classes know nothing of the theatre, and never go to the play. In this country, you do not hear workmen singing or whistling airs from the operas, as do our workmen, who all have their favourite actors on the Boulevards. The lower orders work, spend their money in beer and gin, and die in the workhouse or the gutter, without ever having dreamed of the existence of art. The middle classes have no taste for the theatre, and the aristocracy only go to kill an evening and yawn their heads off. Intelligent people stay at home.

Besides, theatres are private enterprises, and receive no subvention from the State. The proprietor, who is generally the principal actor of the company, receives little or no support from the others. Even in the best theatres the two principal characters are good or passable ; the rest are worthless. There is no school of declamation, nothing corresponding to our Conservatoire. An actor in this country serves his apprenticeship before an uncomplaining public.

The result of all this is that literary celebrities do not seek to be famous as playwrights. Alfred Tennyson, the English poet-laureate, has written a drama and two comedies, but they only met with a *succès d'estime.*

Actors know best what the public like. They generally give them plays of their own manufacture, which are for the most part translations of French ones. All our plays reappear here mutilated ; and in what a state, to be sure ! *Adapted from the French to suit English taste !* What taste ! What adaptations !

Some are original. Would you like to see with what sort of bait John Bull is caught? I extract from the newspapers of the month of October, 1882, the following Drury Lane advertisement. The name of the play is " Pluck " :—

"69TH PERFORMANCE OF PLUCK.

"PLUCK—Genuine Fun.
" PLUCK—Thrilling Scenes.
" PLUCK—Loudest Joy.
" PLUCK—Saddest Grief.
" PLUCK—ever witnessed.
" PLUCK—in three hours.

"69TH PERFORMANCE OF PLUCK.

" Return of AUGUSTUS HARRIS, the greatest Actor
—Author—Manager, since the days of
David Garrick.

"69TH PERFORMANCE OF PLUCK.

" Gigantic Success.
" One hundred thunders of applause.
" Two hundred roars of laughter.
" Marvellous effects.
" The greatest success of the season."

All this is literal. It is not all either. This gentleman thus appeals through the papers to the British public, whom he caters for, and has taken the measure of, I must say : " Let every man—good or wicked, every woman—virtuous or otherwise, fallen even, come and see my play. Instead of following in the steps of those who have made thieves and cut-throats sentimental heroes who die ' babbling of green fields,'

I have shown how, even in this world, crime, treach-
ery, and falsehood, although triumphant for a time,
must in the long run have their day of reckoning.
I shall endeavour in the future, as I have in the
past, to prove worthy of the great trust and responsibility reposed by you in me. Under my direction,
Drury Lane Theatre, the National Theatre *par excellence*, will ever be a school of morality."

All this beats Eno's Fruit Salt.

In this single play, there are besides assassinations
and robberies, a railway accident, a fire, a storm,
and the sacking of a bank, the windows of which
are smashed to atoms.
Good Mr. Augustus! Lucky spectators!
Is it not sickening?

I will content myself with giving you one more
of the kind : it is the advertisement of the Surrey
Theatre, a second-class house.

" *Surrey Theatre*.—Seven acts of realism.—Five
thousand persons had to be refused admittance on
Saturday last; the omnibuses had to stop on account
of the vast MULTITUDE that were turned away. Those
who were fortunate enough to obtain seats, gazed in
breathless excitement at unparalleled scenes. Horror
and delight were alternately written on their coun-
tenances. Never was virtue more triumphant, never
was vice more confounded than in this vast theatre."
A little farther on you read : "The most inhuman,
simious, horrible, blood-curdling, terrible, savage,
weird, fantastic, human, unearthly, fiendish, fasci-

nating, repulsive, and attractive play, ever produced
or ever imagined.—To commence at half-past seven
precisely."

In a grand spectacular play entitled "*Waterloo*"
I saw the famous John Shaw killing his eleven
Frenchmen. The complaisance with which those
eleven unhappy lancers advanced one after another
to be exterminated by the terrible Life-guardsman
deserved a better reward.

However, there are some serious theatres in
London. During the season, that is to say from
April to August, the best musical talent in the
world is to be heard in Covent Garden and Drury
Lane, where the works of the greatest composers of
foreign opera are given.

The only English theatre really worthy of note is
the *Lyceum*. Mr. Henry Irving is a talented actor,
who studies his parts conscientiously. He is very
good in drama, and, though the English Press have
been rather severe at times in their criticisms of
his Shakespearean impersonations, he must nevertheless be acknowledged to hold the first place upon
the English stage, and to be the only successor of
Garrick, Kean, Kemble and Macready.

In England, there is no national theatre corresponding to our *Théâtre-Français;* nor is the want
of such a house felt. Shakespeare's plays are the
only ones that would be available for its repertory.
The theatre of the Restoration is coarse, and most
plays written by the dramatists of that time are
founded upon comedies of Molière: Wycherley,
Congreve, and Farquhar only wrote for the licen-

tious mistresses of Charles II., and the people of
the nineteenth century, still so puritan, would have
to stop their ears.

Sheridan, it is true, wrote two remarkable comedies : " *The School for Scandal* " and " *The Rivals ;* "
but no more.

It is a strange and remarkable fact, even for this
country of contrasts, to have produced a Shakespeare and to have the national repertory begin and
end with his creations : Shakespeare, the king of
poets, inimitable, unapproachable, a sort of demi-
god—and after him utter sterility ! " Indian Empire,
or no Indian Empire," says Carlyle, "we cannot
do without Shakespeare ! Indian Empire will go,
at any rate some day ; but this Shakespeare does not
go ; he lasts for ever with us ; we cannot give up
our Shakespeare."

For the past three years, our excellent actors of
the *Comédie Française* have given performances at
the Gaiety Theatre during the month of June.

Society flocks to hear them. It is very much to
be doubted whether John Bull is capable of appre-
ciating our Coquelin. But that does not matter
at all. When John has paid his guinea, he enjoys
himself, even if he does not understand a word, as
the following anecdotes will prove.

Madame Modjeska, a Polish actress, who has
successfully played several of her principal *rôles* in
English at the Haymarket and Court Theatres, had
been asked to play in a large London drawing-room.
She was besought to recite a poem in her own language. " But," said she, " you will not understand

me, and I like to be understood." The company insisted so much that she at last yielded, and, striking
a tragic posture, recited something in Polish. John
and his guests were lost in admiration. Next day,
everybody knew that Madame Modjeska had given
them, as a recitation, the numeral adjectives from *one*
to a *hundred*.

Madame Sarah Bernhardt made a provincial tour
a few months ago. The day that she was expected
to play at Blackpool, she was taken with a severe
sore throat. She went to the director of the theatre :
"I shall not be able to play to-night," she said to
him ; "I have lost my voice."—"What does that
matter?" said the impresario, who thoroughly understood his patrons ; "the people want to see you ;
you need not speak, only gesticulate, they will be
equally well pleased."—"But I am not an exhibition ; I am an artiste," replied the celebrated actress
indignantly. Sarah is obstinate ; to the great disappointment of the director she neither played nor exhibited herself.

Mrs. Langtry, a lady mixing in the highest society,
and one of the handsomest women in England, which
is saying a great deal, went on the stage in the early
part of this present year. After having played or
rather shown herself to the London public about a
dozen times, she went to America. All the American newspapers agree in saying that she has no talent
for the stage, but the Yankees flock to see her, and
pay from ten to fifteen dollars for an orchestra stall.
The English newspapers have telegrams every day
giving all particulars of the great financial success
of her visit. The Prince and Princess of Wales sent

her their congratulations. The amusing part of it is, that, while Mrs. Langtry draws crowded houses at fabulous prices, Madame Adelina Patti, who is also in New York, plays to comparatively empty benches.

The three solemn knocks which, in the *Théâtre-Français*, precede the rising of the curtain, are unknown in England. Here, a polka or a quadrille is inflicted on you between each act of *Hamlet* or *Othello*. On the other hand, you are not annoyed by the obsequious attentions of a box opener. Of the two evils I prefer the quadrille, inasmuch as it is included in the price of the ticket, and, moreover, you can go and smoke your cigar whilst it is being administered to the house. Another good thing about English theatres: the intervals only last a few minutes, and at eleven o'clock you can go home to bed; you deserve it.

XX.

Pianos—Drawing-room Music—Concerts—Oratorios—Musical
Festivals.

In London there is not even a cobbler but has a piano in his back parlour. If people lived in apartments here as they do in Paris, Bedlam, Colney Hatch, and all the other madhouses would never contain the lunatics that the pianos would send them. As it is, everybody has his house, and the evil is not so great.

Every woman, I might say without exception, plays the piano ; but in a private room I have never heard a lady or a young girl play well enough to afford pleasure to a serious amateur. They play without the least expression. One of my compatriots and friends, a distinguished professor and composer, who teaches this instrument of torture in a great London ladies' college, complained one day to the head-mistress that his pupils played without any feeling or expression. "Monsieur," answered the lady with a kind smile, "I did not engage you to teach sentiment to my young ladies."

It is the same with singing. You sometimes come across pretty voices, but they make no impression upon you ; it is nothing but noise. Not a movement, not a muscle of the face relaxes ; it is a mechanical action of the vocal chords, a mere physical phenomenon.

I was one evening in a drawing-room. A young lady who had travelled in Italy and studied music there, was asked to sing. She sang, and indeed with a good deal of taste, the pretty song by Arthur Sullivan: "Let me dream again."

"That young lady sings very well," I said to a lady at my side.

"Ye—es," she replied, with a little pout of scorn; "but how affected she is, rolling her eyes, and putting her hand to her heart! All those gesticulations are highly ridiculous and very improper. One would think she was an actress."

The English, who know what awaits them in the drawing-room, have such an appreciation for chamber music, that the very sound of the piano is the signal for general conversation. When the piece is finished, the company leave off talking, and reward the amateur with a "Thank you."

Punch, who knows them, represents *Herr* Bogulobuffski in the act of executing a piece on the pianoforte. Seeing that everybody is engaged in conversation, he pauses, and says to the mistress of the house: "I hope I am not in the way, and that I do not disturb conversation."

"Oh! not at all," replies Mrs. Ponsonby de Tomkyns; "pray go on."

Public concerts, on the other hand, are excellent, and always well attended. All the greatest singers in the world can be heard in London. The orchestra of the Crystal Palace is perfection. The popular concerts of classical music at St. James's Hall,

10

the Richter concerts, those at the Albert Hall, Co.
vent Garden, the Floral Hall during the season,
cannot be surpassed.   There you can hear Patti,
Nilsson, Albani, Joachim, Rubinstein, Charles Hallé,
Faure, Nicolini, etc.

"J'en passe et des meilleurs."

John Bull is very attentive at such concerts.   He
listens with all his ears.   You wonder why he does
not listen to *Herr* Bogulobuffski in Mrs. Ponsonby
de Tomkyns's drawing-room.   The reason is that
John is charged a guinea or half-a-guinea at these
public concerts, and that he only really appreciates
that which he has paid for, and paid for properly.

The oratorio flourishes in England . it is the
music for which John Bull shows a predilection.
He likes these biblical subjects set to music.   Look
at him in his stall (profanation ! I should say in his
pew) ; he does not move, his eyes are closed, that
he may hear the better, just as he closes them when
he listens to a sermon.   He is happy ; it looks as if
he had come to church.   The oratorio is for him a
foretaste of the delights that await him in the next
world.   At the Crystal Palace, he gets his oratorio
with choruses of five thousand voices.   The more
there are the better he is pleased.   "Oh !" exclaimed an Englishman who sat near me at one of
these divine services, "the Italians are all very well,
but for oratorio you must have English singers, you
know."   I am quite of his opinion, just as to make
pastry you must have paste.

It is true that some of these oratorios contain

splendid passages, and that a great number of them were written by such men as Haydn, Handel, Bach, and Mendelssohn. But it is a rather curious fact that most of them were composed in England by these great masters ; perhaps under the influence of the spleen ; it is Thames fog set to music.

An oratorio lasts from three hours to three hours and a half. In the country, at the great musical festivals of Bristol, Hereford, Leeds, and Birmingham, oratorios are given every day for a whole week, beginning with the *Creation*, and so on through the list : *Abraham, Joseph,* * *Elijah, Judas Maccabæus*, the *Messiah*, the *Martyr of Antioch*, by Arthur Sullivan, the English Offenbach, the *Passion*, *St. Paul*, etc., etc. The English will not be happy until the whole of the Bible is set to music.

---

* The indignation, with which Joseph rejects, in B flat, the improper propositions of Mrs. Potiphar, is epic !

XXI.

LONDON alone possesses three hundred and fifty
newspapers, about fifty of which are devoted to re-
ligious questions and news : The *Christian*, the
Christian World, the *Christian Herald*, the *Christian
Chronicle*, the *Christian Era*, the *Christian Review*, the
Christian Globe, the *Christian Age*, the *Christian
Union*, the *Christian Life*, the *Catholic World*, the *Prot-
estant Times*, the *Protestant Standard*, the *Universe*, the
Baptist, etc. : the vocabulary will soon be exhausted.

The *Daily News*, the *Standard*, and the *Daily Telegraph* are the papers that you see, in the morning,
with a few exceptions, in the hands of every Englishman who can afford this little penny luxury. These
papers consist of eight large pages of seven or eight
columns each. Five whole pages are devoted to advertisements. The reason is that, in this country,
everything is obtained by advertising. The Universities, the great Institutions, are compelled by their
statutes to make known through the papers, that
such and such a chair is vacant. For instance, you
will see such advertisement as the following : " *University of London.*—The chair of Sanskrit is vacant.

Emoluments *so much*.   The candidates must send in
their applications, accompanied by testimonials, on
or before such and such a date."

Every one advertises for what he wants : professors, journalists, authors, governesses, cooks.   Even
lovers appeal, through the papers, to a faithless mistress or a fickle sweetheart.   In order to attract attention, the latter advertisements are placed at the
head of the first column on the first page.   I copy
some of these heart-rending appeals :—"A. M. to J.
C. K.—My darling, do not leave me any longer in
anxiety.   I eat no more ; I sleep no more.   Whatever has happened, I forgive you, and kiss your
sweet face.   Come."   The next is a little bit less
romantic : "To William F. R.—Why did you not
keep your appointment with me ?   I am dying to
see you.   Send P.O.O. to the same address as before."

The daily papers of which I have just been speaking are colossal enterprises.   The correspondence
and the telegrams, which sometimes cost ·fabulous
sums, are beyond anything of the same kind that
can be seen on the Continent, where each newspaper belongs to a political personage, whose opinions it represents.   The *Standard* is the organ of the
Conservative party, the *Daily News* that of the Liberal party.   But, if the correspondence and the telegrams of these leading English papers are superior
to those of Parisian papers, the articles are much
inferior.   Nothing is more dull, more devoid of interest, than the leaders of the great political organs.

Thanks to the liberty of the Press, journalism is a
formidable power in England.   On the other hand

the journalist himself is not an authority as he is in
France.   Articles are not signed, and outside the
fraternity nobody knows, or cares to know, the name
of a single writer of the *Times* or any other paper.

The king of all the newspapers of the universe is
the *Times*.   Its sixteen pages, eleven of which are
devoted to advertisements, appear every morning,
and cost threepence.   This paper, the reputation
and influence of which have been greatly overrated,
does not belong to any political party.   It is a creak-
ing old weathercock, as a friend of mine called it,
which one sees every morning throwing its venom
right and left, to the general terror of continental
newspapers, which exclaim : " The *Times* says this,
the *Times* says that."   This sheet of advertisements
and police news, which pretends to know the ·secrets
of all the European Cabinets, including those of the
Maison-Dorée, has no other aim but money-making ;
and if it represents any interest at all, it is that of
the great city bankers.   With the exception of the
Jerome Paturots in search of a social position, who
pore over the advertisements of the *Times* in read-
ing-rooms, the clubs, and other public institutions,
the great mass of the people does not read this en-
vious, pedantic, and nagging old journal.

Punch, the London *Charivari*, is a little weekly
paper, full of fun and humour, showing that it is
possible to be witty without ceasing to be refined.
The caricatures are admirable, and the best of them
is that no mother would think of forbidding her
daughter to look at them.   I open at hazard :—" I
say, papa, are you still growing ?" says a pretty little
girl to a papa whose baldness seems to be taking

alarming proportions. "No, my dear; why?" "Oh! because your head is coming through your hair!" Farther on it is a political skit. Lord Beaconsfield, then at the head of the Government, has got the Sultan of Zanzibar over to London. "Well, now that your Highness has been able to see what a civilized nation is like, I hope, on your return to your country, you will give orders for the suppression of the slave trade." "I shall do my best, my friend; only I must tell you that the Conservative party is very strong over there."

And the caricatures of the great statesmen! You should see how *Punch* handles them, and uses them as stock-in-trade! In his character of jester, he takes all manner of liberties with perfect freedom; his innocent hits are sure to be taken in good part.

There is no limit put to the liberty of the press in this country. Everything is reviewed and criticised by the papers, and not infrequently in the plainest, most violent terms. Sentences too severe or too lenient, political and administrative acts, everything has to pass through the Caudine Forks of a severe criticism. There is not a judgment, not a decision, that need be considered as oracular. Public opinion is the supreme court of judicature. I do not suppose there was ever a voice raised in England to propose that a restraint should be put upon the liberty of the press, which in a free country is the correlation of the sovereignty of the people.

Press offences, properly speaking, there are none. Offences committed through the columns of a newspaper are treated as common law offences, and punished as such.

Everybody, in England, can read, and does read. The most insignificant village cobbler has a little library, or, at least, a few books on the table of his modest parlour. We must of course except the lower classes of London ; but they are quite a distinct population, such as you will find in no other part of the country. In France, the labourer's wife has her old missal ; but it is in Latin : of what use is it to her? In this country, these worthy people all have their Bible, written in a language both simple and lofty ; all have read it, and will read it again.

The absence of books among the middle classes of France is striking. Working classes are satisfied with reading the *nouvelles diverses* and the sensational novels of the *Petit Journal* ; it is with such literature that our ordinary *bourgeois* feeds his mind. Every Englishman, I repeat, has a library : besides, he generally subscribes to a circulating library, which supplies him, for the sum of a guinea a year, with as many novels as he can digest.

England has produced, during the last three centuries, a succession of literary monuments that only ancient Greece and France are in a position to admire without envy. A list of princes indeed. In poetry—Chaucer, Shakespeare, the immortal bard, Spenser, Marlowe, Ben Jonson, Milton, the "mighty-voiced inventor of harmonics ;" Dryden, Prior, Pope, Gay, Young, Thomson, Burns, Thomas Moore, Walter Scott, Cowper, Byron, Shelley, Keats, Tennyson ; in history and philosophy—Bacon, Locke, Gibbon, Newton, Addison, Swift, Goldsmith, Samuel Johnson, Hume, Smollett, Burke, Hallam, Macaulay, Grote, Carlyle ; in fiction—Fielding, Sterne, Cooper, Walter Scott, Lytton, Disraeli, Charles Dickens, Thackeray, Charlotte Brontë, George Eliot.

Ainsworth and Anthony Trollope have just died ; and it seems as if we must expect a time of rest, or sadder still, of decadence. Shakespeare has attained heights which it does not seem possible for man to approach ; Milton made blank verse perfect. These messengers of the gods have passed away ; they will return no more. In Germany—Goethe and Schiller ; in Italy—Tasso, Ariosto and Dante ; in France Corneille, Racine, Molière, Voltaire, and Victor Hugo ; in ancient Greece—Homer, Æschylus, Euripides, and Sophocles ; so many heroes—demi-gods ! Like the Messiah, they came with a message to the earth. That message is delivered, and they will come no more.

The English modern novel is not, like the French one, a picture of the improbable, but a true picture of everyday life. Thackeray, the English Balzac, has painted the aristocracy of his country ; the inimitable Dickens, the middle and lower classes ; George Eliot has dissected the human heart ; between them they have left little unsaid. Here, a novel can be put into the hands of youth without fear of its warping the mind, and such is the moral tone of the greater part of English fiction, that few parents concern themselves about the novels that their children read. A boy can, in all security, take a novel to school without fear of its being confiscated. In France, a boy in whose desk a novel of Alexandre Dumas, or perhaps even of Erckmann-

Chatrian had been found, would be relentlessly ex-pelled.

The English are fond of the fine arts, and are ex-cellent connoisseurs. How could they be otherwise, admirers of Nature as they are? The land of Joshua Reynolds, Turner, Hogarth, and Landseer, possesses at the present time a legion of talented artists: Frederick Leighton, Millais, Alma Tadema, and many others.

The knowledge of drawing is more widely spread in England than in France. You will generally find in the house of an English gentleman the illustrated diary of the travels of some member of the family. Every well-educated girl can sketch a landscape. Who has not seen them on our Normandy beaches and hills, pencil and palette in hand?

The picture galleries, with which Pall Mall and Bond Street abound, are the rendezvous of English good society. You can pass a delightful hour in these rooms, which sometimes only contain about half a dozen pictures. One of the most frequented is the Doré Gallery. The great French artist, whose pictures, so powerful, so vivid, have made him uni-versally popular, and whose loss France still mourns, was very much appreciated in England. His great religious pictures—the *Crucifixion*, the *Martyrs*, the *Ascension*, *Christ leaving the Prætorium*, *Ecce Homo*, the *Entry of Christ into Jerusalem*, the *Dream of Pi-late's Wife*—have attracted vast numbers of people for the last ten years.

The following is a list of the principal picture galleries :—

Society of British Artists.
City of London Society of Artists.
Doré Gallery.
Dramatic Fine Art Gallery.
Dudley Gallery.
Dulwich Gallery.
French Gallery.
Grosvenor Gallery.
Society of Lady Artists.
National Gallery.
National Portrait Gallery.
Royal Academy.
South Kensington.
Society of Painters in Water Colours.
Institute of Painters in Water Colours.

These picture galleries are open to the public all the year round. There exist many others, of less importance, to which the public are only admitted during certain parts of the year.

XXII.

To develop the physical faculties of the young, and
by means of liberty and confidence to cultivate in
them the love of what is right, such is the double
aim of the great English schools. They would
have educated men, but, above all, they would have
men, vigorous men, strong in body and in mind.
Mens sana in corpore sano.

Therefore, no barrack system ; fresh air in abun-
dance, open fields and long free walks. No other
policemen or watchdogs than conscience and public
opinion. Each pupil is expected to be in his place
at the time for classes or meals, and in his place
each is to be found. What temptation is there to
play truant ? After school hours, the English
schoolboy may do as he likes, and go where he likes.
When we, poor prisoners, could evade the porter's
vigilance, and run to the tobacconist's shop across
the road to get a pennyworth of tobacco, we felt like
perfect heroes of romance. On our return, our
schoolfellows flocked round us to sniff a little of the
fresh and free air that we had breathed for a moment. The cigarette .is never seen in the great

centres of English education. If it were forbidden as strictly as it is with us, it would soon be just as popular in England as in France. It is a kind of savour of forbidden fruit that makes smoking attractive ; freely permit it, and it loses all its charm.

Eton, Harrow, Rugby, Marlborough, Wellington, all the greatest schools, are in the country. They are regular little towns, with parks or fields around them instead of courtyards. London possesses only five of these institutions : St. Paul's, Westminster, Christ's Hospital, Merchant Taylors, and City of London School ; and even the first-named of these is to be transplanted next year to an immense piece of ground in the suburbs.

A head-master, in spite of his five or six thousand a year salary, is not an inaccessible potentate ; quite the contrary, he knows personally every pupil. All the faces are familiar to him. And not only the faces, either, for young boys are still caned in English schools ; it is one of the privileges of the head-master : every unruly boy is taken to him to receive this chastisement. M. Taine makes the observation that no head-master of a French *lycée* would lower himself so far as to whip a pupil. That is all very well ; but the English are practical before everything. By expelling a boy for the least infraction of discipline, as is done in France, you blight his future. Here, he gets two or three strokes of the birch, and there is no more said about it : *pêch! puni est tout-à-fait pardonné.* The boy may not boast of it, but neither will he consider himself disgraced ; the treatment generally has a salutary effect, and the culprit is received back into the good graces of his masters, and continues his studies as if nothing had happened.

In the public schools, no routine, no advancement according to seniority—that premium offered to stupidity in France. When a pupil gets too advanced for his class, the head-master promotes him to a higher one. In sixth forms, which correspond to our *classes de rhétorique*, you will sometimes find boys of fourteen or even thirteen. In France, there are students of higher mathematics who do not know their first book of Euclid, *Rhetoricians* who do not know their declensions. Here, each class is composed of from twenty-five to thirty boys, no more. They all have to be attentive, and all profit by the lessons given by the master, because he can give every boy individual attention.

The classes in French *lycées* are composed of ten pupils of extraordinary capacities, who are prepared for the *grand concours de la Sorbonne*, of about twenty who follow the lectures anyhow, and of fifty poor boys, neglected, forgotten even, who learn nothing, who are mere wallflowers.

In England, none of those thousand petty offences made up to annoy and irritate young people. I remember to have had, *en Rhétorique*, five hundred lines of *Athalie* to copy for having asked the boy sitting next to me to let me dip my pen in his inkstand.

In England, an intelligent boy costs his parents nothing to educate. He easily obtains a scholarship by competitive examination. When his studies are finished, he can obtain from his school an exhibition worth eighty or a hundred pounds a year for the four years that he means to pass at Oxford or Cambridge. At the same time, he can try for another scholarship at the University of his choice, and thus take up, for four or five years, a sum of about two hundred pounds. Each public school has its own income, administered by a council of governors. All these institutions for higher education are their own mistresses, and each is independent of the other.

Public school boys get on very well among each other. The dunces are not despised as they are with us. On the other hand, the hero of the English schoolboy is not the top boy of his class, but the quickest runner, the best athlete. At Eton, the school for the aristocracy, the heroes are first the young noblemen, next the sons of rich parents: the ones that are looked down upon are the foundation scholars, otherwise the cleverest boys. Still lower in the scale come the masters, I am told. A French schoolboy always feels inclined to lift his cap when a scholar who has carried off a prize at the great Sorbonne examination passes near him.

Each school has its clubs: Athletic sports club, football club, cricket club, debating societies. All these societies have their president, their treasurer, their secretary. Nothing is wanting. The headmaster and other masters are honorary president and vice-presidents; but the pupils alone generally attend the meetings. One of them acts as president, and perfect order reigns throughout these little parliaments. The secretary takes notes and draws up the minutes of the meeting, which are read at the

opening of the following one. In the debating societies, all sorts of questions, literary, political, and
social, are gone into.   I saw one day, when I visited
St. Paul's School, that the question to be discussed
at the next meeting of the Society was "Women's
Rights : ought woman to play a political part in the
commonwealth?"   The names of the speakers who
would support or who would oppose the proposition
were given.   When all have had their say, the president counts the ayes and noes of the voters.   These
young fellows thus get accustomed early to express
themselves well, to speak in public, and to be one
day ornaments of the House of Commons.   Never a
rude or improper word is heard in these meetings.
Everything is carried on in a calm, dignified manner.
They are held after the masters have left the school
house.   No mistrust, no watch kept, no police.   It
is a perfect government.   The maintenance of order
is in the hands of the citizens.

Each large school has its magazine, edited by the
most competent scholars of the upper forms.   These
periodicals, which indeed are very interesting, give
all the news of the school, accounts of the meetings
of the different societies, literary articles, and poems,
and are read by the pupils and ex-pupils, whom it
keeps informed of all that is going on in the place
where they passed some of their happiest days.
These publications tend to keep up a pleasant intercourse between old schoolfellows, and to strengthen
the *esprit de corps* amongst them.
    I think, on the whole, too much importance is at-
tached to athletic games.   I cannot make up my

mind to admire those legs and biceps that are tried and betted upon exactly as at a horse race.

I admire the development of the physical faculties; but I draw the line at professional runners and walkers. I prefer a horse. Many of the games are very dangerous. Football is a wild game fit for savages. Picture to yourself fifteen great fellows on either side of a large ball that has to be kicked through the two goals of the opposite side, pushing and bustling, rolling over one another at the risk of getting their ribs or jaw-bones broken, breathless, their clothes torn, their shoulders lacerated, their hair on end, their faces covered with perspiration, blood, and mud; their eyes blackened perhaps, but glowing with excitement, for all that is nothing to compare to a defeat. "Fine game, sir!" remarked to me a sturdy young fellow, the first Latinist of a large school, who had just won a victory over the fifteen players of another public school. "It was rather hard work; but we have beaten them all the same. They cannot play against us; they haven't any wind." Hundreds of spectators, ladies as well as gentlemen, gather round the lists, and applaud and encourage the players with their shouts and bravos. Others besides schoolboys take part in these savage games: officers, gentlemen—every active man of England plays football.

Football and cricket are the two national games: the former is played from the first of October to the first of April, and the latter from the first of April to the first of October. Cricket, a much quieter game than football, and very interesting when one understands the rules well, consists in aiming a

leathern ball at three sticks planted in the ground,
and defended by the adversary armed with a flat
club which serves to return the ball far enough away
to allow him to run between the two lines of sticks,
until the ball has been retrieved. Such are the
games over which young England goes wild and
intoxicates itself. In spite of accidents, which occur
too often, it must be admitted that such pastimes
are preferable to the reading of *Nana*, or to conver-
sations often obscene that are carried on in our college yards.

To show to what an extent the confidence placed
in an English schoolboy is carried, I must tell you
that a master will not unfrequently say to a class :
" I shall expect you to bring me your translation to-
morrow, done without using a dictionary or gram-
mar. I should like to see how you will be able to
manage it." No head-master would take the liberty
of opening a letter addressed to one of his pupils ;
the result of this system of confidence placed in them
from their tenderest years is, that at fifteen years
old, English boys know how to behave themselves
like men. The English coolness of manner is admirably calculated to frustrate children's artifices ;
no raising of the voice, no displaying of temper,
which only irritates them, and which they know
how to take advantage of if you do but give them
the victory over you, by showing them that they
possess the power of putting you out of temper.
The empire over one's self, self-control, that eminently English virtue, is the quality most essential to
a schoolmaster. I know nothing less enviable than

the position of a master who cannot make himself respected by those merciless little tyrants called schoolboys ; it must in the long run produce disastrous effects upon the brain.   I read the other day, in a newspaper, that a pupil had by his insolence and sarcasms driven his master to shoot himself.   I should have shot the young rascal, I know.

After having spoken so highly of the great public schools, what language shall I use to give an idea of those two great centres of learning in England, the Universities of Oxford and Cambridge ?   Oxford especially ; Oxford with its twenty colleges hundreds of years old, its museums, its rich libraries, its lawns, its parks, its gigantic trees covered with luxuriant foliage, its towers clad with ivy, virginia creeper, honeysuckle, and clematis, its long shady walks like cathedral naves.   Everything around you has an air of classic sanctity, and inspires in the heart, ideas of poetry, study, and peaceful seclusion.   It is in the shade of these gigantic oaks, on the richest verdure that Nature ever offered to the eyes of man, under the shadow of these venerable walls, the very stones of which have a history, that the young Englishman finishes his studies.   One cannot look at these impressive sights without being mentally carried back to France, without thinking of our poor, solitary Sorbonne so gray, so cold ; of our students living in wretched lodgings in the *Quartier-Latin*.

No women of evil repute in Oxford, I am told ; the authorities see that the young men under their care have liberty combined with freedom from danger.   When the students are not at work, they are

at the great club of the university—the Union.
There they have all they require : reading rooms,
coffee, and billiard rooms, studies, libraries, gardens,
and also the great hall, in which the members meet,
under the presidency of one of their number, to discuss the questions of the day. In the summer, they
are on the river, in hundreds of boats, and each
wearing a boating costume, with the arms of the college to which he belongs.

Living is expensive at Oxford, and a student cannot keep himself on much less than three hundred
pounds a year ; but, as I have said, the cleverest live
at the expense of their colleges and of the public
schools in which they were educated. A volume
would scarce suffice to give a description of the
treasures that are contained in this unique town.
The Bodleian Library alone would require many
pages devoted to it. It is there that is kept the
most ancient manuscript of our old national epic of
the eleventh century, the *Chanson de Roland.* It was
my privilege to see and touch this precious little
volume that some of our troubadours carried about
in their pockets : I could not help feeling deep emo-
tion as I opened it.

Oxford has still the reputation of being a centre
of prejudices in religious matters. " Oxford, famous
for dead languages and undying prejudices," once
said Mr. John Bright. Cambridge is more liberal
and less aristocratic. It was Oxford that burnt Lati-
mer and Ridley. Macaulay reproaches her with it :
" Cambridge had made them," he said ; " Oxford
burnt them." It should be added that Macaulay
was a Cambridge man.

The University of Oxford was founded in the ninth century by Alfred the Great, and that of Cambridge dates also from the middle ages. England possesses several other universities : London, Durham, Manchester, and others ; but they are of modern foundation, and do not enjoy such a reputation as their two time-honoured sisters.

Oxford and Cambridge are the nurseries of the great men of England, and it would be difficult to say which of the two has produced the greater number : perfect harmony exists between them, and they give each other mutual encouragement in the path of labour and honour. All the clergymen of the Church of England have studied at Oxford or Cambridge. Therefore they are at once well-educated men and gentlemen. They marry and become useful members of society. The young vicar is very much sought after in the higher classes : he has only to choose a girl and throw the handkerchief, and she is his.

The two great Universities appear in public, once a year, on the Saturday preceding Holy Week, to the enjoyment of the London populace. The Oxford and Cambridge University Boat Race is, after the Derby, the most important event of the year for the betting world. For a week everybody wears, in his button-hole, a dark blue (Oxford) or a light blue (Cambridge) ribbon. The contest takes place on the Thames, near London. The two boats are each rowed by the eight best oarsmen of the University, who for months have been in special and hard training.

Here, as in the public schools, the popular heroes

are the best oarsmen, cricketers, and football players. Oxford and Cambridge also have contests at football, cricket, and billiards.

The debating societies of the great public schools and universities have formed the greater part of the best orators of England. Canning, Gladstone, and a hundred others, made their *début* in the *Union*. These gatherings, which might give a lesson in good order and courtesy to our legislative assemblies, were formerly held, at Oxford, in a little narrow lane, that may still be seen in the neighbourhood of Wadham College, and which is called *Logic Lane*. There the antagonists used to encounter to discuss important questions of philosophy. When they could not succeed in confuting their adversaries, they knocked them down. This way of proceeding was called the *argumentum baculinum.* " It was their method in these polemical debates," says Addison, " first to discharge their syllogisms, after the manner of Socrates, and afterwards to betake themselves to their clubs, till such time as they had one way or other confounded their gainsayers." This puts one in mind of the time when the universities of Europe were divided into Greeks and Trojans. The latter bore a mortal enmity to the Greek language, and Erasmus tells how he had the misfortune to fall one day into the hands of a party of Trojans who beat him and left him in the street for dead.

XXIII.

To become a lawyer, doctor, or officer, you must pass examinations. To become a schoolmaster, it is quite unnecessary : you open a school for boys or girls, just as you would open a grocery shop. I know of a tailor who, having failed in business, has set up a school in my neighbourhood ; he is getting on finely. In every street, at every step, you see on a door a brass plate with the inscription : *Establishment for young gentlemen,* or *Establishment for young ladies.*

Education is uncontrolled by any authority. The establishments in question are not subject to inspection ; but the pupils who are sent to them are generally well fed and allowed time for play ; the rest the parents do not trouble themselves much about.

The other day I received two prospectuses, from which I will give you a few extracts. I keep the style intact ; it would be profanation to touch such *chefs-d'œuvre.*

"*Terms as low as possible to keep schools select and secure thorough teaching.*

"*They are examined every July by a gentleman from*

the College of Preceptors, thus combining the advantages of a Public with a Private School.

" Meals if wished. Luncheon and dinner, 9d. Tea, 4d.

" Terms include English only. French, music, walks, extras.

" Being very fond of babies, eighteen months to two years is preferred for their admission.

" The religion of parents is never spoken against, but the Bible must be taught.

" Quarter from day of admission, hoping parents will thus never lose time, as it is advantageous on account of the examinations to enter at once. Thorough teaching. No cramming allowed."*

The second prospectus was accompanied by a list of rules to be observed by the pupils. This list seems to be an exercise upon the different tenses of verbs. You shall see for yourself.

First comes the future :

" 1. When you hear the bell at six o'clock, you will get up immediately."

The next is in the conditional ·

" 5. If you should talk at table, you would not get any pudding !" (*sic*).

Then comes a subjunctive :

" 14. It is required that you should never be seen without a cravat in class or at table."

To conclude, there is the imperative :

" 20. If you do not feel very well, go to Mrs. H." (Mrs. H. is the worthy wife of the head of the school.)

---

* I beg to say that the original prospectus is in my possession.— MAX O'RELL.

A friend of mine, a schoolmistress, had a plate put upon her door, with the inscription : *Establish-ment for young ladies.* Her landlord, a builder, promptly appeared, furious. "Take away that plate immediately," he said to his tenant ; "I let you my house as a private dwelling : you are de-stroying all the privacy of the neighbourhood, and my house property will go down."

"But you have a plate upon your* own door," remarked the lady.

"I know that," replied the builder ; "but my business is respectable, at any rate."

Among the shopkeeping classes, the word *school-master* raises a scornful smile.

The words *teacher, tutor, governess,* are for them synonymous with *poor devil, broken-down folk.* Eng-land owes this to her indifference towards education, and to Charles Dickens, who, in his writings did his utmost to lower the dignity of the schoolmaster. His intention was to chastise those thousands of ignorant men who kept schools, ill-treated the children, caned them unmercifully, and saved appear-ances by going about in a long black coat and a white neckcloth. But he went too far, and the people see Wackford Squeers in every school-master.

You may read every day in the newspapers advertisements like the following :

"A cook wanted ; wages £25."

"Wanted, a governess, able to teach English, French, drawing and music ; salary £20."

It is merely board and lodging that the gener-ality of advertisers offer to a governess :

"A comfortable home offered to a governess who would be willing to undertake the education of three young children." No mention of salary.

Proprietors of private schools usually procure their teachers through a scholastic agency.

When you require a place as tutor (*place* is the word employed), you apply to a scholastic agent. No need to produce any diploma or certificate; you state what you know, and what you can teach; that is all that is necessary.

I know a young Frenchman who one day applied to one of these gentlemen. "I shall not be able to find you a place, sir, unless you undertake to teach some other subject in addition to French," said the agent to him. "Can you draw?"

"Yes, a little; I think I could give elementary drawing lessons."

"Elementary!" exclaimed the agent: "do not say elementary. You teach drawing; very good. Do you play the piano?"

"I could play *Au Clair de la Lune*, and I can read my notes pretty well."

"Very good. Don't you think you could play the *Marseillaise*? The *Marseillaise* is a great favourite in this country."

"With one finger, perhaps."

"You will do capitally; I engage you; I shall write to the schoolmaster to-day; make your preparations for starting to-morrow."

He did start the next day, and what is more surprising than this singular interview, is that my young friend suited admirably.

I myself have had some small experience of the scholastic agent. About ten years ago, I obtained through the medium of an agency an interview with a Yorkshire schoolmaster, who, as you will see, wanted a gentleman who could make himself thoroughly useful.

I told the reverend gentleman (for he was a clergyman) that I wished to perfect myself in the English language ; that I was ready to teach French to his pupils ; that I did not expect a large salary, but should require a little time to myself for study. On hearing the words : *I do not expect a large salary*, the reverend gentleman smiled, evidently a smile of satisfaction. "I offer you thirty pounds a year," he said to me, "board and lodging ; you will only have your laundress's bill to pay."

"Will you kindly tell me what my duties will be ?" I inquired.

"We get up at six. You will have to look after the boys while they dress, and you will stay with them in the schoolroom until breakfast time at eight o'clock. After breakfast, you will take them for a walk till half-past nine. The morning classes are held from half-past nine to one o'clock. The subjects that I shall expect you to teach are Greek, Latin, French, mathematics, drawing, music, and dancing : English history and geography I teach myself."

At this prospect of having to teach the piano and the mazurka, I grew reflective, but I begged the gentleman to continue.

"At one o'clock we dine," he resumed, "and at two, the afternoon classes begin, and last till five

At five we have tea. After tea, you will take the
boys out walking until seven. From seven to eight
you will see that they prepare their lessons for the
following day. At a quarter-past eight, we partake
of bread and butter or cheese, and at half-past eight
the boys go to bed."

" They have richly earned it," thought I.

I rose to take my hat, and was about to politely
take leave of this constructor of well-filled time-
tables, when he stopped me and smilingly inquired :
" Couldn't you also teach a little German ? "

" With pleasure, I'm sure," I said ; " but what
time should I have to cook the dinner ? " And, without waiting to see the effect that my remark must
have produced upon the man, I left cured of the
scholastic agency for ever.

A few weeks later, I engaged myself in the school
of a worthy man who consented to make me work
three hours a day only, on condition that I should
require no salary. I left him at the end of a month :
his wife, who got drunk every Saturday, one day
threw a pot of beer in my face.

I resolved to give up teaching, and went as a
boarder to a school where I was to pay eight pounds
a month. This school enjoyed a very good reputation : the French master was a Swiss ; the piano was
taught by a German, singing by an Italian, and the
piano-tuner was a Pole : Noah's ark on a small scale.
I knew English tolerably well by this time : at the
end of a few months, I could write and speak it to
my satisfaction ; I was thinking of leaving. My new
master probably guessed my intention, and one fine
morning took me aside and said to me " You speak

English very well ; I should advise you next, if you
wish to perfect yourself, to teach French to English
pupils ; it will enable you to compare the two languages better, and, if it is your intention to take up
teaching as a profession, it will be excellent practice
for you. If you like, I will allow you without chang-
ing our money arrangements, without your paying
anything extra, to practise upon my own pupils."
It was easy to see what this clever man of business
wanted to do : he would send away the Swiss, and
instead of having to pay a French master, by this
plan he would have one who would pay him eight
pounds a month.   It was quite clear and very clever.'

I had been upon the point of teaching my native
language for thirty pounds a year ; I had taught it
for *nothing* a year ; now I was in danger of having to
pay for teaching it ; the situation was getting tragic.
I ran and packed up my traps. *Je cours encore.*

The under-master in these schools is a drudge,
especially the French one.   He must, before all
things, meet the approbation of the scholars.   Woe
betide him if there is a decision between himself and
one of the pupils to be made.   A child who leaves
is not easily replaced ; competition is too great : but
he, poor fellow, if he had to go, there would be ten
others ready to fill his place the day after.   He
knows it, and puts up with the ill-treatment of these
merciless young rascals.   If the pupils insult him,
or cannot be made to work, he makes no complaint,
all the blame would fall upon him.

The principal himself never has anything but
praises for his pupils.   His reports to the parents
are admirable.   If he were to say that a boy was not

making progress, the parents would take their child away the term after.   If he complained to a father of the want of intelligence in his boy, he would be told that he was paid to give him some.

As a rule, in England, when a pupil is successful in his studies, it is put down to his intelligence and hard work ; when he is lazy and learns nothing, it is owing to his having a bad master.

Charles Dickens, in his preface to " Nicholas Nickleby," thus expresses himself upon the subject of private schools : " Of the monstrous neglect of education in England, and the disregard of it by the State as a means of forming good or bad citizens, and miserable or happy men, private schools long afforded a notable example.   Although any man who had proved his unfitness for any other occupation in life was * free, without examination or qualification, to open a school anywhere ; although preparation for the functions he undertook was required in the surgeon, in the chemist, the attorney, the butcher, the baker, the candlestick maker, the whole round of crafts and trades, the schoolmaster excepted ; and although schoolmasters, as a race, were the blockheads and impostors who might naturally be expected to spring from such a state of things, and to flourish in it, the Yorkshire schoolmasters were the lowest and most rotten round in the whole ladder.   Traders in the avarice, indifference, or imbecility of parents, and the helplessness of children ; ignorant, sordid, brutal men, to whom few considerate persons would have entrusted the

* He is still.

board and lodging of a horse or a dog. . . . . I make mention of the race, as of the Yorkshire schoolmasters, in the past tense. Though it has not yet finally disappeared, it is dwindling away."

Very slowly, I might add.

A young Frenchman of my acquaintance went to spend a month in a provincial school, to learn a little English and teach a great deal of French, for no salary I need not add. The day after his arrival, the following advertisement appeared in the paper of the neighbouring town : " Mr. R., assisted by resident and visiting masters, gives a thorough education at moderate charges." My young compatriot happened to be the only assistant master of the establishment ; but he was *resident*, since he resided in the house, and he could also be said to be *visiting*, as he was only on a visit. So there was nothing absolutely untrue about the puff.

English people are very great upon words ; lying is unknown. I was one day travelling with an English bishop. We were five in the compartment. On arriving at a station, we heard a cry : " Five minutes here!" My lord bishop immediately began to spread out on the seats travelling bag, hat-box, rug, papers, etc. A lady presented herself at the door, and asked : "Is there any room here ?"   " All the seats are occupied," replied the bishop.

When the poor lady had been sent about her business, we called his lordship's attention to the fact that there were only five of us in the carriage, and that, consequently all the seats were not engaged. " I did not say that they were," answered my lord : " I said they were *occupied*."

XXIV.

THANKS to the barrack—I had almost said prison—
system practised in our *lycées*, French boys are Re-
publicans, Radicals, Socialists. They dream wild
dreams of liberty, they gasp for freedom, revolu-
tionary heroes are the heroes they worship.

Youth, alas! is a complaint that does not linger
about us long. How many of those red-hot Radicals
I knew in my schooldays now sing *ora pro nobis* in
the street processions of the Holy Virgin!

English boys, who enjoy the most complete freedom at home and at school, are ultra-Conservatives.
Their patriotism makes them so. The Liberals have
the reputation of aiming at reforms; now, to admit
that reforms are wanted, is to admit that England is
not perfection, and it would be difficult to persuade
her youthful sons that such was the case.

You will hear English people say, "Conservative
as an undergraduate."

The greater part of these young men are sons of
noblemen or of country squires.

The squire, as a rule, is nothing out of the common
in the way of intellect : he has only his birth to thank
for the position he occupies. His days are passed

in eating and drinking, smoking and hunting, and taking up his rents. It strikes him as very strange that there should be people who are not pleased with their lot. "What discontented people there are in the world, to be sure!" he exclaims, as he reads in his newspaper the account of a strike or a manifestation in favour of such and such a reform. Reforms indeed! He considers that things are very well ordered in this best of worlds.

The squire is the magistrate of his parish; he is in the commission of the peace. A poor beggar tried to excuse himself one day before his squire, by exclaiming, "I must live, your honour."

"I do not see the necessity for that," replied the magistrate, indignant at such presumption.

The Universities of Oxford and Cambridge, which each send two members to Parliament, are represented by Conservative landlords or manufacturers. The Liberals, it is true, present their most distinguished professors as candidates; but they are almost ignominiously defeated. This is how: To be an elector of one of these Universities, it is sufficient to have lived three years at Oxford or Cambridge, and to have obtained the degree of Bachelor of Arts, which, three years later, is changed for that of Master of Arts, merely upon the payment of certain fees. So all these sons of gentlemen leave college with the degree of B.A. ; with this difference, it must be explained, that, while part of them are bachelors of first, second, or third class, the others are not classed at all. The former become professors, barristers, etc. You find them in after life occupying the highest positions. The latter return

12

home to shoot over papa's property or go into the
Church.   Bachelors with honours and bachelors
without honours are in the proportion of one to six.

This is why, at the University elections, the Conservative candidate wins by such a large majority.

An English *savant*, member of the University of
Oxford, and a staunch Conservative, told me one day
that he always refrained from voting for his *alma
mater*, because, said he, "The Conservative candidate I don't like ; and I cannot accept the political
opinions of the Liberals."

I know another, also a great scholar, and also a
Conservative, who invariably votes for the Liberal
candidate.   " It is a preposterous thing that our
great centres of learning should be represented in
Parliament by noodles of country squires, or big
tradesmen !"   Whenever he has to vote, he sacrifices
his personal opinions to the honour of his University.

London University, the students of which belong,
as a rule, to Liberal-minded families, sends a Liberal
representative to Parliament.   They generally choose
a *savant*.   A few years ago, it was Mr. Robert Lowe ;
at present it is Sir John Lubbock, the banker,
naturalist, and philanthropist.

The Chancellors and Rectors of the Universities
are dukes, marquises, or earls : it is the Marquis of
Salisbury at Oxford ; the Duke of Devonshire at
Cambridge ; Earl Granville in London.   If you happen to be born a lord in England, you are born a
legislator, diplomatist, artist, learned man—anything
you like.   In Figaro's time, the nobleman could
play the guitar from his birth : that was more wonderful still.

XXV.

Of all methods of making itself conspicuous, the court of St. James's has adopted the most economical : that of being conspicuous by its absence. The Queen does not spend more than a fortnight of the year in London. She passes four months at Balmoral, in the midst of her farmers ; three months in a very simple country house in the Isle of Wight, and the rest of her time at Windsor. She gives two balls and two concerts a year at Buckingham Palace, in London. This palace is now scarcely inhabited, except by rats ; and the Empress of Russia, who passed a month there in 1875, suffered terribly from rheumatism all the while. At all the receptions the Prince of Wales and his charming Princess replace the Queen. They do it admirably. Amiable, and ungrudging of their trouble, all the year round they may be seen journeying hither and thither, laying foundation stones of churches or other important buildings, opening hospitals, bridges, colleges, piers, etc.

The Princess of Wales, mother of great sons almost old enough to be married, but with a sweet, ever-girlish face, is the idol of the English people. You see her portraits in the shop windows, taken with a little cat in her arms, or her baby on her back : that will tell you what she is. Impossible to be other than good with such a face as that.

I know of no position in this world more enviable than that of Her Britannic Majesty : the deep attachment of a great nation, the empire of 300,000,000 souls, the finest royal domain in the world, little or nothing to do, complete security, magnificent revenues, and not the slightest responsibility.

The Court is more German than English : the Queen give posts and places in it to most of the German Princes whom Prince von Bismarck has relieved of the care of their own states. It is thought that the Prince of Wales will change all this one day. The Queen has married her daughters to Germans : the eldest will be Empress of Germany ; the second was married to the Grand-Duke of Hesse Darmstadt (she died in 1878) ; the third to Prince Christian of Schleswig-Holstein, who lives at the expense of John Bull. The Duke of Connaught married the daughter of Prince Frederick-Charles and the Duke of Albany the Princess of Waldeck Pyrmont, to whom the English Parliament allows a grant of six thousand pounds a year.

The rest of the German Princes are generals, admirals, governors of the Queen's castles, etc. They are very inoffensive, for that matter, and never harmed anybody, not even Her Majesty's enemies.

One of the most formidable is His Serene Highness Prince Leiningen, late captain of the Queen's yacht. His duties consisted in crossing the Solent

four times a year, a voyage of twenty minutes' duration. He managed, on one occasion, to run down a
sailing boat in broad daylight, and drown three persons, who were imprudent enough to cruise in the
same waters as this experienced navigator. This
most serene fresh-water sailor drew a salary of
£2,000 a year, and has lately been promoted to the
grade of rear-admiral

There are two great political parties in England
—the Liberals and the Conservatives : the rest are
perfectly insignificant ; a change of ministry is ef-
fected in a few hours. When a newly elected House
of Commons is not composed of the same elements
as the one which it replaces, when the majority has
become the minority, the Queen dismisses each minister, and passes their portfolios to their successors.
In this way, the ministries of Disraeli and Gladstone
have alternated every six years, for almost a quarter
of a century. It is very seldom that a ministry remains in power more than six years : John Bull
likes to give his ministers a change now and again,
as a recompense for their zeal, and devotion to
their country.

The members of the Royal Family are careful to
refrain from talking politics. The Queen's sons are
the leaders of Society, but you never see them at a
political meeting or dinner. They abstain from voting in the House of Lords, whenever, by giving their
votes, they might be showing the slightest preference for either party.

The late Prince Albert once took the liberty, at a
public dinner, to allude to politics. The papers of

the following day handled·him so severely that he
was quite cured, and never ventured on the subject
again. The Englishman likes everybody to keep his
proper place, and I feel convinced that, if the Royal
Family were to take it into their heads to meddle in
politics, their days in this country would be num-
bered.

A political career is a thankless one. The Queen's
sons keep clear of politics, and they are well inspired
to do so : thus they keep their prestige. They are
the first gentlemen of England, received with acclam-
ations in public, in private as free as the humblest
of Her Majesty's subjects. Their path is not strewed
with crackers, and when they go to bed, they have
no fear of finding boxes of dynamite under their
pillows. Lucky Prince of Wales ! Poor Czar of all
the Russias ! So long as there is a monarchy, there
will be one in England : a monarchy capable of giving lessons in liberty to more than one Republic.

The existence of the House of Lords is an insult
to the common sense of the English nation. The
nobility is here essentially a moneyed nobility, a monopoly of property, which the law of primogenitureship, only existing in the aristocracy, concentrates
into a few hands. Nine-tenths of the English peers
would be unable to produce any quarters farther back
than the last century. The heroes that are ennobled
are heroes of money ; English pale-ale and double-
stout have more earls and barons to answer for than
all the other national products.

The seats in the House of Lords are hereditary,
and there is always a crushing majority on the Con-

servative side. But the House is not destitute of common sense, and knows quite well that its existence entirely depends upon its keeping quiet and not attracting public attention.

The two legislative bodies never clash, and yet, when the Liberals are in power, the Lords could throw out all the bills passed by the Commons. They take care to do nothing of the kind. No matter how radical a measure the Commons may pass, the Lords do not reject it. They begin by making a little opposition, it is true; some young viscounts may go so far as to talk about their independence, but it does not last long; the few able and clear-sighted members in this venerable assembly are there to give the key-note.

The leader of Her Majesty's opposition generally terminates the debates with an allusion to his patriotic desire to do nothing that shall disturb the peace of the country he loves. He will give his vote, he says, although doubting very much whether the law in question is going to benefit the nation. He only hopes it will not do too much harm and resigns himself. The day the House of Lords rejects any important measure passed by the L'berals, it will have dealt its own death-blow.

The two great political parties are of about equal strength. The result is, that the Opposition always united, well directed, and well disciplined, is formidable. It acts the part of a break upon the wheels of the Ministry's chariot. Everything the Government proposes is condemned in advance; every war it undertakes is unjust, and every treaty of peace it signs is cowardly. If a battle is lost,

the Government has all the blame to bear; if a
victory is won, it is thanks to the bravery of the
army.   It never has done and never can do
anything worth praising.   But the task of the
Government is relatively an easy one, in all im.
portant questions they can rely on their majority;
not one will desert them.   No parliamentary groups
to be humoured, because they possess the power of
menacing the existence of the Ministry at every
turn.   When a Liberal wishes to absent himself for
a session, he tries to find a Conservative who is
desirous of doing the same   They pair off, and in
the event of a division, the absence of neither
gentleman gives the majority to his opponents.
The Irish party, however, grows more national every
day, and the Government may, before long, have to
reckon seriously with it.

The most perfect order reigns throughout the
House of Commons during the debates.   The
Liberals and Conservatives respect and esteem each
other.   Personalities are impossible, thanks to the
excellent system which obliges every orator to
address his remarks to the speaker, and never to
call any member by name.   "Sir," a member will
say to the speaker, "the honourable member for
N. wishes to know whether I," etc.; or, "the noble
lord, the member for N., is labouring under a delu-
sion," etc.

The room is small and rectangular ; the two parties sit facing each other, and with their hats on ; a
member only bares his head while he is speaking.
No tribune to mount: in front of the speaker is a
table ; each orator, as he wishes to speak, approaches

it, and, with his back turned to his own party, speaks, not to the House, but to his opponents, whom he seeks to convince, without ever succeeding, it is needless to add. *Parliament* signifies "a place where one talks," from the French *parler.*

If the English member of Parliament is calm and strictly parliamentary in the House of Commons, he is nothing of the kind in the meetings at which he addresses his constituents. There he is violent, without a fear of being called to order for the expressions he uses ; he denounces his opponents in the plainest terms. At such meetings I have heard Gladstone spoken of as an old villain, a hoary-headed scoundrel and traitor, a miscreant abandoned of God and man. Disraeli as a Venetian Jew, a Jerusalem donkey. The right honourable gentlemen were none the worse for it.

In the spring of 1883, one of the larger evening papers thus expressed itself on the recovery of Her Majesty from a sprain : "Her Majesty has had a serious accident, there is no disguising the fact ; but the prayers of an entire nation have succeeded in obtaining from the Providence that watches over our beloved Sovereign, an earlier convalescence than we dared to hope for. The recovery of Her Majesty will bring back joy to every fireside, and happiness to the heart of every true-born Englishman ; it will put an end to those moments of solemn anxiety which, alas ! have already been of too long duration."

No one has a greater respect and admiration than myself for Her Majesty, and the feelings of deep-rooted affection she inspires in her people ; but *two whole* columns of abject platitudes, on the subject of a sprain, will prove that the ceremony of kissing hands is not the only exercise of the kind which cer tain subjects of Her Britannic Majesty indulge in.

XXVI.

If you would keep a really lasting impression of St. Petersburg, visit it at the time of the year when, to save your nose from freezing, you must rub it with snow every five minutes.

If you would keep an impression of London that nothing would efface from your memory, come and see it on a Sunday, and, if possible, let it be one Sunday when there is a good east wind blowing.

All the shops are closed; not a creature stirring; miles of deserted-looking streets everywhere; the gray houses and the gray sky seem to meet and mingle. Around and above, look where you will, the same sad tint encircles you and strikes chill to the marrow of your bones. It gives you cold shivers.

Here and there you may see a few roughs leaning, pipe in mouth, against the walls of the public-houses, waiting for the doors to be opened. These dens are only opened from one o'clock to three in the afternoon, and from six to eleven in the evening, on Sundays. At a quarter to eleven, in the morning, the bells begin to ring. The sound of these bells is harsh and extremely irritating. I have asked and been told the reason why peals of bells are scarcely ever heard. The churches, built about *as strongly* as the houses, would never stand them.

Now you see a sight that the English say excites the envy of the whole world : the English nation going to church or chapel. Each one carries his books in his hand ; a Bible, a prayer-book, and a hymn-book. The bigger these books are, the better it looks. Some are of great size, and they are carefully displayed as much as possible. They have not to be carried far, it is no superhuman task, the churches are about as numerous as the public-houses, and everybody has one close to his door.

We will not enter the churches just yet. we will reserve that for a special chapter.

The' service concludes at half-past twelve or one, and the English nation then returns home to dine. The evening service commences at seven.

During the interval the English nation takes a nap. The fathers and mothers, half asleep in their easy chairs, take a few nuts and a glass of port. No visiting on Sundays. The children read the Bible or the true stories of some wonderful conversion out of a tract, that has been left at the door by an agent of the Bible Society.

A good Englishman never goes out during church time. If he does not mean to go to church, he alleges a slight indisposition as an excuse. There are very few who admit that they are not church-goers ; there are none that boast of it.

One Sunday morning, whilst I was on a visit to an English family, I proposed a walk. A son of the family offered to accompany me. As we were leav·

ing the house, he noticed that I had taken my walking stick. "Take an umbrella," said he ; "it looks more respectable."

Those agents of the Bible Society, with their tracts, are terrible bores. You meet with them in omnibuses, in trains, in the streets, everywhere. With a hypocritical smile they beg you to accept a tract. Your best plan, if you would quickly have done with them, is to accept the piece of paper, put it in your pocket, and say : "Thank you." I met with one once who made quite a dead set at me.

"Sir," he began, "God commands every man to repent."

"I thank you for reminding me, but I had not forgotten it," I said.

"Ah ! sir, you are a foreigner ; seek salvation, save your soul, whilst you are in this country."

"Have you the keys of Paradise, then ?" I asked him ; "and is that your calling to bother people in this manner ? Leave me alone."

"Sir, believe me, all men are sinners. David himself was one."

"I agree with you," I exclaimed.

"Yes, but he repented."

"There was room for repentance."

"The repentance should make us forget the crime."

"Exactly. But why, then, do you hang your criminals?" I added, for I was beginning to be amused at the turn the conversation had taken.

"Because, by executing them, whilst they are in a state of repentance, we send them to Paradise. If we set them at liberty, they would return to a state of sin."

"Now, tell me," said I to him, "for you seem to be an intelligent man, would you receive in your house, at your table, with your good wife and children, a man who had caused the death of another in order to make love more easily to his wife, but who had afterwards repented? Would you not welcome more warmly one who had never had occasion to repent of such crimes as those of David?"

"Ah!" he replied, "your levity is out of place. Laugh at me, if you like ; we shall see in the end who will be on the laughing side. We shall meet again at the Last Day." After giving me this appointment he left me, with a look more jeering than Christian, I am sorry to say.

I have often heard that these agents do not make any proselytes, especially among foreigners, in England. I do not believe a word of it. I could tell of some wonderful conversions myself. One day I received the following letter :—"Sir, having lost my situation in France, I came over to England, where I have gained an honest livelihood for several years past. These explanations will make you as well acquainted with my private life *as I am myself.* Since my arrival in England, I have completely changed my ways. I know the Lord, I have become a Protestant and a total abstainer. Unfortunately, I am now in bad health. Compatriots in a foreign land should help one another, and if you would lend me a few pounds, or even one, you would oblige me greatly, and I should be exceedingly thankful to you. Be kind enough to receive, with my anticipated thanks, the expression, etc."

Among the other Sunday heroes, the street preach-

ers must not be forgotten. They are generally con-
ceited workmen, who, having received from Heaven
a mission to go and convert their fellow-creatures,
relate their experience of life to the public : how
they were once nothing but miserable sinners, how
they have seen the error of their ways and become
converted, and how easy it is for others to do likewise. They take up their stand in some open place,
in parties of five or six, accompanied by one or two
old maids. Here, more than anywhere, old maids
offer to God that which they have had no chance of
giving to men : a pure and loving heart. A circle
is formed, and a monotónous hymn sung : this is to
attract the passers-by. One of the party steps forward, takes off his hat, collects his thoughts in it,
and commences his discourse. The theme never
varies. "My dear friends, death is at hand : are
you prepared to meet it ?" A crowd soon gathers
round silent and respectful. It is not a religious
silence, but a simple mark of that boundless respect
which is entertained in England for the liberty of
meeting. The men smoke their pipes and listen ;
it is the only distraction to be had on Sundays, so
they avail themselves of it. They do not pray, but
on the other hand, neither do they mock. The sermons are dull twaddle, and generally full of personal
experiences. "My dear friends," said one of these
street evangelists, "I am happy to be able to say
that I am saved, that I am now on my way to
Heaven. A month ago, I could not have said this,
I was the slave of the devil." Indeed, it was easy to
see he was telling the truth, for *le diable sur son nez
avait marqué ses exploits.*

The only street orators, who are occasionally amusing, are the agents of the Temperance Society. They, I quite believe, do some good. They speak to the workman in language that he can understand ; they relate anecdotes. The audience are allowed to ask questions, to raise objections ; answers are always forthcoming. " Here, I say, I've got something to say to you, just listen a minute," said one of them to a ragged workman, who was listening one day at a meeting of this kind. " You carry your money to the publican, who makes you drunk every day, don't you ? You and your wife and children starve, while the publican has his joint of beef, or rather *your* joint of beef—for your money paid for it—roasting under your nose ; only look at your worn-out boots : who is there that would give twopence for everything you have on your back ? I am a workman like you ; but look at my good strong boots ; there, look at my warm woollen waistcoat, look at my overcoat. To-day, when I go home, I shall find a good dinner ready ; it isn't the publican, it's my missus that cooks it. I drink water, that explains the difference. Why don't you do the same ? "

" What ! " replied the man thus harangued, " cannot a man take a glass with a friend ? "

"Yes, to be sure. Drink one, if you like; but if you are not satisfied with one glass, sign this pledge, as I did, and bind yourself to drink nothing but water."

These people, thus abruptly appealed to, do not lose their temper. Some reply with a laugh, "Well, old fellow, you can drink water if you enjoy it. I am off to drink a glass of grog to your health." I have seen others go to the register and sign.

These missionaries are not all completely disinterested. Some of them make a fine income by preaching temperance. I know of one, an American, who wanted fifteen guineas for delivering half-an-hour's address at the Crystal Palace. The same individual asked for a hundred and fifty-five pounds for himself and his wife, who were wanted to preach temperance at Brighton for ten days: and, what is still more astonishing, is that he got it.

The Americans are business-like people. For that matter, foxes will fare well so long as there are geese to be plucked.

John Bull will never be able to be very proud of his Sabbath so long as the public-houses are kept open on Sundays. There exist fifteen hundred thousand persons in London whose existence is a problem, and whom no church seeks to attract to itself. The aristocracy, the upper and lower middle classes, all go to church and chapel; the lower classes go to the tavern and get drunk. "Let us close the public-houses on Sundays," cry the Liberals and the philanthropists. "Let us keep them open," cry the Conservatives, bishops, and archbishops in their van. "Our museums, picture-galleries, theatres, concerts, everything is closed on Sundays," said a Conservative to me. "We have our comfortable homes and clubs where we can pass the day without finding the want of other attractions; but the people of the lower classes, living in wretched hovels, what distractions have they? It is to our own interest, moreover, to leave them the only one they possess and appreciate. So long as they are stupefied with drink they will give us no trouble. The day we close the

13

public-houses of London on Sundays we shall have
a terrible revolution."

Ay, terrible indeed! One look at the faces of the
women and men who frequent these drink-shops
will persuade you how terrible. The thought makes
one shudder.

Bible or beer ; Gospel or gin : no other choice on
Sundays ; no intermedium in this country of contrasts.* It is, as M. Taine says, " Paradise or Hell :
no Purgatory in England."

Children must not play on Sundays. I once saw
two little creatures of six or seven playing with
oranges in the street. A gentleman went up to
them and gave them a severe reprimanding for their
naughtiness. Old maids are terrible on Sundays ;
woe be to the children who fall into their clutches on
the Sabbath !

In France, blind beggars play the flute. In England, they read aloud from a Bible printed in raised
characters, over which they pass their fingers. I am
inclined to suspect more than one of them of knowing a chapter of Jeremiah by heart, and of calmly
reciting it, whilst sprawling their fingers over the
pages for form's sake.

You will see the walls of all waiting rooms covered

---

* " In Kilburn, a most respectable suburb of London, there are
25 places of worship and 35 public-houses. On November 26th,
1882, between the hours of six and eight in the evening, 5,570 persons entered the places of worship, and 5,591 the public-houses."—
Daily News. "A Public Worship and Public-house Census at
Kilburn."

with sheets of scriptural texts printed in large type. Go to the most private places for men, you will see in front of you, "God sees thee," or "Make haste; God waits for thee." Turn which way you will, Bible here, Bible there, Bible everywhere.

Prince Bismarck, who, it appears, has a remarkable talent for whistling, landed at Hull one Sunday. "I had just set foot for the first time on English soil," he related. "I began to whistle as I went along the street. An Englishman stopped me and said: 'Sir, be good enough to stop whistling.'— 'Stop whistling? What for?'—'Because it is forbidden. It is Sunday!' I made up my mind not to stay in Hull another hour, and I started for Edinburgh." Poor Prince Bismarck! What an inspiration! Fancy going to Scotland to escape from the form of tyranny that is called in England the observance of the Lord's Day! Scotland, the land of John Knox and the cradle of Puritanism! Bismarck has never boasted of the success he met with as a Sabbath Day whistler in Scotland.

XXVII.

In France, Catholics go to church, Protestants to
their temples, and Jews to the synagogue.

In England, members of the English Church go
to *church*, members of dissenting sects go to *chapel*.

That which strikes a stranger, as he enters English places of worship, is the total absence of poor
people. I make an exception, however, in favour of
the Catholic churches.

The English Church, who counts among her followers the aristocracy, the well-to-do classes, and
about half of the middle classes, all of them believers in the doctrine that the other world will be
peopled with all sorts and conditions of men, yet
none of them anxious to commence acquaintance,—
does not seek to attract the poor. You never see a
shabbily-dressed person in a church, especially not in
a London one. The pastor takes care that his flock
shall be in good company.

As to the dissenting churches or chapels, their
reason is a different one. The English Church is
supported by the State, but each chapel is kept up
at the expense of the faithful. The ministers live

upon subscriptions, collections, presents, and invitations to dinner. Here again the uselessness of the poor is, alas! only too apparent.

Divine service is always conducted in English, and consists principally of extracts from the Bible, and of hymns. More than half the service is passed in singing, very loudly and terribly out of tune. Rowland Hill was anxious to see an improvement in church music. He did not see, he said, why Satan should have the sole privilege of listening to good music. It is certain that the Creator does not hear much in the English churches, except, perhaps, in the cathedrals.

The manner in which the faithful kneel is rather remarkable. The prayer-book contains very precise directions on the subject, however; it even employs a tautological phrase which it is impossible to interpret in different ways: "Here the congregation shall kneel on their knees."

But the faithful kneel on something else; they sit down; then, with their elbows on their knees, the upper part of the body thrown forward, and their faces buried in their hands, they look, from a certain distance, as if they were all on their knees. Not a bit of it. They are cheating; they are all comfortably seated.

The service commences with the general confession. The whole congregation joins in this general examination of the conscience, this universal confession, a confession all the more convenient that there is no need for each sinner to specify his sins; it is the same confession for the greatest sinner as for the most innocent child: "We have left undone those things which we ought to have done, and we have done those things we ought not to have done." Very easy and convenient, as you see. John, in his religion, as in all other matters, throws overboard everything that is inconvenient, or that might prevent his career from being rapid and prosperous.

The confession over, the pastor gives the absolution. This moral cleaning being thus concluded to the general satisfaction, the troop of spotless lambs begin to express their sense of relief in all manner of keys.

The service terminates with a sermon, a very short sermon, which rarely lasts more than a quarter of an hour. As every one attends the church he likes best, and as there are many to choose from—Heaven knows how many!—it is politic to render the service agreeable. The sermon is generally a very ordinary production of the mind, and rendered still more tiresome to listen to by being read. " How do the Church of England clergy think I am going to remember their sermons, when they cannot remember them themselves?" said a Presbyterian friend to me one day. This practice of reading a sermon is accounted for in the following way: the members of the English Church differ upon certain questions of dogma, and a clergyman may preach a sermon that is displeasing to his flock. If complaint were made to the bishop of the diocese, the clergyman might be called upon to produce the sermon in question. That is why he writes it, and reads it from the pulpit. I see another explanation of the practice in the following advertisement : " For sale fifty sermons at moderate prices. Apply, by letter, to *Clericus*, Post Office, Manchester."

I find in *Punch* the following skit : "Ah! sir, what wicked people there are in the world!" says a worthy old woman to her vicar: "they say you stole your sermons."

"Tell them it is not true, my good woman. The sermons are mine. . . . I paid for them."

The Catholic Church, with cathedrals, cardinals, archbishops, bishops, and a numerous clergy to support at her own expense, is obliged to turn everything to account in order to make the two ends meet.

On Sundays, after service, the Catholic churches give concerts. These concerts are advertised in the newspapers, along with the theatres. You pay sixpence in the central nave, and threepence in the side seats. On grand occasions, when there is to be a solemn procession through the church, with a bishop in the rear, the prices are doubled : seats are a shilling, and sixpence. You receive a ticket on entering, just as you do at a theatre. These concerts are all the more patronised because on Sundays there is no competition. Besides, some of them are excellent : there is a full orchestra, singers, and every attraction.

The British public puts itself quite at its ease at these concerts ; you see that it has come to church to hear some music. It is rather peculiar to see the assembly turn their backs to the altar, so that they may face the orchestra, which is usually placed in a gallery, over the main entrance.

I once accompanied to vespers, at the Catholic cathedral of Southwark, a lady with strongly pronounced Protestant views. When she saw the or-

chestra and the lustres blazing with light, the poor
lady was all bewildered : "Do you think," she whis-
pered to me, when we were seated, "that I should
look ridiculous, if I were to say my prayers?"

I must say that the services at Westminster Abbey
and St. Paul's Cathedral are very imposing : the
chants are splendid, simple, but grand. The sermons
are preached by the greatest orators of the Anglican
Church.

In the dissenting churches, the prayer-book is dis-
pensed with ; no liturgy is followed. The minister
conducts the service unaided : he prays for the congregation, gives out the hymns, preaches a sermon,
and concludes by passing round his hat. The pro-
ceeds of the collection are for him ; they are his fees.

The collection is the hinge upon which the service turns ; the *clou*, as we should say in French the-
atrical slang. In France, the collection is made in a
deep bag ; in England, the thing is managed more
cleverly: a little salver is used. He who would be
capable of putting a button into a bag, feels bound
to display a piece of silver on a plate that is passed
to him. The collector himself, on emerging from
the vestry, places a few half-crowns and other silver
coins on the plate, just as a consulting doctor places
a sovereign on his desk : it is to tell you, "That is
what is expected of you." When you go to mass in
France, you must be there in time for the Gospel or
it does not count ; in England, you must be there before the collection. In England you will never find
a clergyman committing the blunder of having the
collection made at the door, after the service, when
every one is in a hurry to go, and very few pay any

attention to the bag that is held out to them. Whilst you are all in your places, the plate is passed in front of you ; your right hand neighbour presents it to you, and you, in turn, pass it to the person on your left, and so on to the end of the seat, where the collector takes it, in order to hand it on to the next row of seats. Impossible to close your eyes and pretend to be asleep, as French church-goers are liable to do, when the priest simply rattles his bag at the end of the pew.

The following English joke is stale, worn-out : Two shipwrecked sailors are just giving up all hope of being rescued. "What can we do to recommend our souls to God?" says one of them ; "we do not know any prayer ; we do not know any hymn : what in the world could we do?"

"Let us make a collection," suggests the other.

XXVIII.

The Religions of England.

If Christianity consists in going to church, and passing one's life in discussing theological questions,
then John Bull is mightily Christian; if piety consists in quarrelling over the dogmas, instead of prac-
tising the principles, of religion, then the piety of
John is unequalled. The craze for religion has come
to a mania. Let the religion be good or bad, no
matter which it is, or what it is, it is better than none
at all. In France, we boast of our foibles, even of
many that are not to be found in us; in England,
people boast of their virtues, especially those they
do not possess. The Frenchman is the braggart of
vice, the Englishman is the hypocrite of virtue.

Here, every religious belief is respected: the Shakers, the Ranters, the Peculiar People, the Salvation- .
ists; Free-thinkers alone are excluded. When a man
wants a situation, he presents himself to his future
master as a Christian; he advertises, in the papers,
as a total abstainer. If, in France, he recommended
himself as a good Christian, he would receive a per-
emptory kick that would send him straight to paradise.

Every Englishman worships God after his own
fashion. There exist here 183 religious sects certi-

fied to the Registrar-General. Each of these sects has naturally found the truth. As, unfortunately, no one has ever yet come back from the other world to tell what he has seen, it seems probable that there are yet many days of peace and plenty in store for the dervishes, the fakirs, and others who live in indolence upon the superstition and simplicity of the world.

Christianity is admirable. Christians are often far from being so. I have more esteem for the Mahometans who follow up their religion. Show me the Christian who loves his neighbour as himself; who, when he has been struck on the right check, holds out his left; who forgives his enemies; who does not ask for that which has been taken from him; who does unto others as he would have others do unto him.

Religion has lost much of its purity and sincerity from ceasing to be private, especially in England, where, owing to competition, to free trade applied to religious matters, every one aims at appearing better than his neighbours. Pray, not standing in the synagogues, nor upon the house-tops, but enter into thy closet and shut the door, say the Scriptures. How many do so?

The Romanists swear by the Pope; the Protestants by Luther and Calvin; the Puritans by John Knox; the Wesleyans by John Wesley; the Salvationists by Mr., Mrs., and Miss Booth; the Baptists of London crowd to the Tabernacle to listen eagerly to every word that falls from Mr. Spurgeon's lips. Some people believe themselves saved, if they can only touch the coat tails of Mr. Moody or Mr. Sankey. I have seen women press the hands of these evangelists, as they passed through the throng on their way to the platform where they were going to preach, and go away happy. When Catholics have the gout, it is to Our-Lady-of-Lourdes, to Our-Lady-of-la-Salette, to *la bienheureuse Germaine* that they go : it is Sainte-Barbe that they implore to protect them from thunder and lightning ; the Deity would seem to play a very secondary part in the religion of all these people.

In England, religion is the idea that absorbs and dominates all others. The prisons and mad-houses are full of religious maniacs.

In France, when we hear of a great crime having been committed, we exclaim : "Where is the woman ?" In England, sift the matter, and you will find a chapel. There are few bankrupts, really worthy of the name, that have not built a church or chapel to win the confidence of investors, and, maybe, also to offer to God a little of that which they had taken from men. On opening my newspaper to-day, I read of an individual charged with fraudulent bankruptcy. A worthy old lady, who had trusted him with stock, states that she had every confidence in the accused, especially since the day when he had refused a box at the Opera, which she had offered him, with the remark that he was happy to be able to say that he had never set foot in such a place.

We all remember the sickening professions of religion that Guiteau, the vile and cowardly assassin of poor President Garfield, made day after day for months.

The United Kingdom possesses two State Churches. The Anglican Church, in England and Wales ; the Presbyterian Church, in Scotland. The State Church was abolished in Ireland in 1869.

The Anglican Church is under the jurisdiction of two Archbishops, the Archbishop of Canterbury, primate of England, and the Archbishop of York, and of thirty bishops. The two archbishops and twenty-four bishops have seats in the House of Lords.

The Scotch Church is under the jurisdiction of a General Assembly, composed of clerical and lay deputies, and presided over by a Moderator elected annually by the Assembly, and a High Lord Commissioner appointed each year by the Crown.

The principal Nonconformist Churches are : the Methodists, the Baptists, the Unitarians, the Congregationalists or Independents, and the Wesleyans.

Out of a population of 81,000,000 souls in the United-Kingdom and the Colonies, 18,000,000 belong to the Anglican Church ; 14,500,000 are Methodists ; 13,500,000, Catholics ; 10,250,000, Presbyterians ; 8,000,000, Baptists ; 6,000,000, Congregationalists ; 1,000,000, Unitarians : and about 10,000,000 belong to different sects of less importance.

I will give a complete list of the hundred and eighty odd religious sects of England, reserving for special chapters those that present features of special interest.

Here is the list :—

The Advent Christians ;

The Apostolics ;

The Arminians, who, contrary to the Calvinists, believe that Christ saved all men by His death ;

The Baptists, who deny that baptism should be received before the Christian has arrived at years of discretion and made a profession of faith ;

The Baptized Believers ;

The Believers in Christ, or Christians who believe that their prayers alone can influence the decrees of Divine Providence ;

The believers in the Divine Visitation of Joanna Southcott, prophetess of Exeter, of whom I shall speak in another chapter ;

The Benevolent Methodists ;

The Bible Christians, or Bryanites, a sect founded in 1815, by William O'Bryan, and who receive the Communion seated ;

The Bible Defence Association ;

The Blue Ribbon Army, whose followers drink no alcoholic drink ;

The Brethren, who practise no rites and have no ministers : they baptize one another. According to them, to preach the Gospel is to deny that the Saviour's work is finished ;

The Calvinists, who deny the real presence ;

The Calvinistic Baptists, who find the opinions of Wesley too Arminian ;

The Catholic Apostolic Church ;

The Christians, owning no name but the Lord Jesus ;

The Christians, who object to be otherwise designated ;

The Christian Believers ;

The Christian Brethren ;

The Christian Disciples ;

The Christian Eliasites ;

The Christian Israelites;

The Christian Mission ;

The Christian Teetotalers ;

The Christian Temperance Men ;

The Christian Unionists ;

The Christadelphians ;

The Anglican Church, itself divided into High Church, Low Church, and Broad Church. The adherents of the High Church, otherwise the Ritualists, adopt the confessional and grand ceremonies in imitation of the Roman Catholics. They do not recognise the authority of the Pope, and can therefore receive the financial support of the State. The Low Church affects an almost Calvinistic austerity, and is very much akin to Dissent. The Broad Church party does not believe in hell, and counts, amongst its clergy, some of the most illustrious names of England. The late Dean Stanley was the brightest ornament of the Broad Church.

The Church of Scotland ;

The Scotch Free Church ;

The Church of Christ ;

The Church of the People ;

The Church of Progress ;

The Congregationalists, who appoint their own ministers, and have no settled form of prayer ;

The Countess of Huntingdon's Connexion, who adopt the Church of England Prayer-Book. This sect was founded in the eighteenth century by Lady Selina Shirley, Countess of Huntingdon ;

The Covenanters, a sect founded in the sixteenth century, when the Protestant Church was thought to be in danger ;

The Coventry Mission Band ;

The Danish Lutherans ;

The Disciples in Christ ;

The Disciples of Jesus Christ. Sect founded by
Mr. Thomas Campbell, who proposed to set aside
all questions of dogma, and to establish the unity of
the Church of the Saviour ;

The Eastern Orthodox Greek Church ;

The Eclectics ;

The Episcopalian Dissenters ;

The Evangelical Free Church ;

The Evangelical Mission ;

The Evangelical Unionists, founded in Scotland
in 1840, by Mr. James Morrison, who proclaimed the
greatest sin to be a want of belief that Christ has,
by His death, saved all men, past, present, or un-
born ;

The Followers of the Lord Jesus Christ ;

The Free Catholic Christian Church ;

The Free Christians ;

The Free Christian Association ;

The Free Church ;

The Episcopal Free Church ;

The Free Church of England ;

The Free Evangelical Christians ;

The Free Grace Gospel Christians ;

The Free Gospel and Christian Brethren ;

The Free Gospel Church ;

The Free Gospellers ;

The Free Methodists ;

The Free Union Church ;

The General Baptists ;

The General Baptist New Connexion ;

The German Evangelical Community ;

The Strict Baptists ;

The German Lutherans ;

The German Roman Catholics ;

The Glassites, a sect founded in Scotland, in the eighteenth century, by John Glass, into which members are admitted with a holy kiss. The followers of John Glass abstain from all animal food that has not been bled ;

The Glory Band ;

The Greek Catholic Church ;

The Halifax Psychological Society ;

The Hallelujah Band, whose services consist entirely of thanksgiving ;

The Hope Mission ;

The Humanitarians, who deny the divinity of the Saviour ;

The Independents ;

The Independent Methodists ;

The Independent Religious Reformers ;

The Independent Unionists ;

The Inghamites, followers of Mr. Benjamin Ingham, son-in-law of the famous Countess of Huntingdon ;

The Israelites ;

The Irish Presbyterian Church ;

The Jews ;

The Lutherans, who, contrary to the Calvinists, believe in the real presence ;

The Methodist Reform Union ;

The Missionaries ;

The Modern Methodists ;

The Moravians ;

The Mormons ;

The Newcastle Sailors' Society ;

The New Church ;

The New Connexion General Baptists ;

The New Wesleyans ;

The New Jerusalem Church ;

The New Methodists ;

The Old Baptists ;

The Open Baptists ;

The Order of St. Austin ;

The Orthodox Eastern Church ;

The Particular Baptists ;

The Peculiar People, who trust in Providence to cure them of all ills ;

The Plymouth Brethren ;

The Polish Protestant Church ;

The Portsmouth Mission ;

The Presbyterian Church in England, founded by the Puritans ;

The Presbyterian Baptists ;

The Primitive Congregation ;

The Primitive Free Church ;

The Primitive Methodists ;

The Progressionists ;

The Protestant Members of the Church of England ;

The Protestant Trinitarians ;

The Protestant Union ;

The Providence ;

The Quakers ;

The Ranters, whose worship consists in jumping and clapping of hands ;

The Rational Christians ;

The Reformers ;

The Reformed Church of England ;

The Reformed Episcopal Church ;

The Reformed Presbyterians or Covenanters ;

The Recreative Religionists ;

The Revivalists ;

The Roman Catholics ;

The Salem Society ;

The Sandemanians, who are identical with Glassites, Mr. Robert Sandeman having been the most
fervent follower of Mr. Glass ;

The Scotch Baptists ;

The Second Advent Brethren, who wait for the
second coming of the Messiah ;

The Secularists, who believe that the affairs of
this world should be thought of before those of the
next, and that religion cannot pretend to the
monopoly of what is good and moral ;

The Separatists, who hold their goods at the disposition of brethren in distress, and refuse to take
oath ;

The Seventh-Day Baptists ;

The Shakers, a sect founded by Ann Lee, who had
a divine revelation, wherein it was revealed to her
that the lust of the flesh was the cause of the de
pravity of man ;

The Society of the New Church ;

The Spiritual Church ;

The Spiritualists, who believe they have inter·
course with the spirits of the other world ;

The Swedenborgians, a sect founded by Emman·
uel Swedenborg, in 1688 ;

The Temperance Methodists ;

14

The Trinitarians ;

The Union Baptists ;

The Unionists ;

The Socinians, or Unitarians, who **reject** the doc
trine of the Trinity, and deny the divinity of
Christ : they differ but little from the Humanitarians ;

The Unitarian Baptists ;

The Unitarian Christians ;

The United Christian Church ;

The United Free Methodist Church ;

The United Presbyterians ;

The Universal Christians, whose belief is, that
God will one day call all Christians to Himself,
whether they have been good or bad in this world ;
that sin does not go unpunished, but is punished in
this life ;

The Welsh Calvinists ;

The Welsh Presbyterians ;

The Welsh Wesleyans ;

The Wesleyans ;

The Wesleyan Methodists ;

The Wesleyan Reformers ;

The Wesleyan Reform Glory Band ;

The Working Man's Evangelistic Mission.

Here ends the list of salvation agencies in England.   If John Bull does not go straight to Paradise
it will not be his fault, as you see.

I will now give a few details concerning some of
these sects that appear more interesting than the
others.

XXIX.

NEW sects are being founded every day. Let an obscure minister discover a new interpretation of some passage of Holy Scripture, he will soon attract a congregation, make an appeal to the pockets of his adherents—an appeal always responded to—and then build his little conventicle. One often receives a circular couched in such terms as these :—" Sir— For some time past the want of a new chapel has been felt in the neighbourhood. The Reverend Mr. X. is ready to undertake the duties of pastor as soon as the necessary funds for building him a chapel have been subscribed." First a little edifice in wood is erected ; then the collections swell, and zinc replaces wood, and, provided the zeal of the congregation does not cool down, you soon see a fine stone church arise on the spot.

London will soon possess a Theistic church, founded by a gentleman who, for four or five years past, has been using every argument in his power to prove that God the Father alone should be worshipped. Funds arrive but slowly, and the gentleman in question feels indignant. " Theism," he says, "has many believers; then why do they not frankly avow their belief, and come to me." It appears he has only collected £6,000, and does not consider it enough for a building that would be worthy of the sect he is called to edify.

There is also being prepared, at the present time, a church of the Holy Apostles, where grand spectacular performances will be given by the aid of an orchestra, professional singers, etc. The altar is to be surrounded by gigantic statues representing the apostles. At the back, in the midst of sombre massive rocks, will shine forth a luminous crucifix. The services will be sung by 200 choristers, accompanied upon stringed instruments, the harp especially. The interior will be illuminated by means of an immense silver gilt cross, at the extremities of which will be electric lamps. It promises to be a grand affair, as you see. The organiser of these fêtes, the *impresario*, is a nice young priest of the Anglican Church, whose good looks obtain for him the admiration of the fairer half of his parishioners.

Of all the religions enumerated in the preceding chapter, the Roman Catholic and Apostolic is the least popular. "No Popery!" is still the cry of the English people. The Quakers, the Jumpers, the Salvationists, the Ranters, none of these alarm them; but a black, shaven priest calls up memories of the stake and Bloody Mary. "A scalded child dreads the fire," say the English. The hatred of popery is pushed to the verge of absurdity. Thus, for instance, Good Friday is considered, especially by Dissenters, as a day of public rejoicing, a kind of

Bank Holiday ; the great thing is to do the very opposite of that which is done in Rome. "This is the
day on which Jesus died : let us spend it in retirement," we say in France. "This is the day on which
Christ saved us : let us rejoice," say the English. In
spite of this, most English people still abstain from
eating meat on Good Friday.

To see Protestantism in all its austerity, you must
go to Scotland ; there Calvinism in all its severity is
practised. You see, in Scotland, trifling is not coun-
tenanced ; nothing is done by halves ; no levity or
frivolity is tolerated. I know a Scotch Presbyterian
minister who teaches the Lord's prayer to his children cane in hand ; each hesitation or mistake is
punished by a good cut across the back of the small
supplicant. In the eyes of these gloomy Christians,
gaiety is to be regarded with suspicion ; a joke is a
sin ; for is it not an act of frivolity ? and must not
every idle word be given account of one day ? The
Scotch are a virtuous people ; a people in earnest,
if ever there was one.

The Mormon Church, so flourishing in America,
admits Polygamy and Theocracy. Not content with
the wives he has had in this world, the Mormon can
also aspire to contract marriage in the next. Indeed,
it is a practice of the Mormon Church to recompense an exemplary life by marrying the defunct to
some great departed soul in the abode of the Elect.
In 1876, a friend of mine paid a visit to Salt Lake
City, and was introduced to a Russian princess, at
present the wife of a Mormon bishop. The following are a few of the impressions which the lady com-

municated to my friend. " My first husband has
been dead twelve years ; he was very good to me,
but, in spite of that, I have no respect for his memory, because he did not treat his other wives with
the same kindness and affection that he showed for
me ; and, according to our religion, a man should
not show a preference for one of his wives. As to
our second husband,—ah ! sir, what a man !—what a
saint ! We do not mourn for him, we envy his lot ;
he sojourns in the realms of the blest ; and, last
year, sir, we married him, in our church, to the
Maid of Orleans."

The Quakers are so named, because of the con-
tortions, which the first followers of the sect gloried
in making, while they worshipped, with the idea of
trembling before their Maker. The Quakers never
kneel except to the Supreme Being. They lift their
hats to nobody, address every one as *thee* and *thou*,
refuse to take oath, and will not serve in the army,
because, according to their belief, war is sinful.
They have no sacraments. This sect, also called the
Society of Friends, recognises no consecration ; any
member may speak in their meetings. Complete silence is observed, until one of these new *convulsion-
naires*, moved by the Holy Spirit, begins to pray and
gesticulate. This sect was founded in 1650, by a
Leicestershire shoemaker named George Fox. Mr.
John Bright, the great English statesman, is a
Quaker : this explains his leaving the Ministry of
Mr. Gladstone, in 1882, when the latter decided on
invading Egypt.

The American Shakers are now the nearest approach to the original Quakers. Their religious service is conducted on this wise :—The men and women range themselves in lines, facing one another, and then clap their hands, jump, and shout, until they fall to the ground, exhausted and breathless. If a new sect, worshipping God by walking on their hands, were formed to-morrow, it would surprise nobody very much. There is nothing to hinder it, and given a church, chapel, or meeting-house, there is no form of worship, however senseless, that may not freely be indulged in, unhindered by law. In this church-going country, it does not matter what your religious belief is, provided you go to some place of worship.

"Why do you come to church?" I heard the clergyman of a little Protestant Church in Devonshire exclaim one day from the pulpit. "I will tell you the reason. Some of you come to look as good as your neighbours, or better; you farmers, my Lord's te t s , come to please your landlord; you tradespeople, to inspire your customers with confidence in you; you young women, to display your new dresses; in fact, you all go to church, because you know you are nowhere, if you don't go to church."

It is but right that, in this volume, treating of the topics of the day, I should reserve a special chapter to the Salvationists, the heroes of the moment.

XXX.

Aux grands maux les grands remèdes. There were
the lower classes to be saved, the people who, as I
have already said, never think of setting foot in a
church. The Protestant church did not want them, the
Dissenters did not want them, the Catholic religion,
with its mystic music and Latin services, would have
produced upon them the effect of a pantomime ; the
street-preachers are monotonous to listen to, and only
attract a few idlers and loiterers : it became necessary to adopt energetic means. Plans were laid
for awakening the fanatic that slumbers, even beneath the humble vest of the lowest Englishman.

For a small consideration, about a hundred
workmen were enrolled ; and then, with the stand·
ard of salvation raised, and drums beating, these
recruits were paraded dancing, jumping, gesticulat·
ing, and shouting along the London streets, to the
amazement and intense amusement of the population.
" Laugh if you like," cried the new proselytes, " you
are going to hell and we are saved ; we are on the
laughing side." And on they went jumping the

higher, and shouting the louder : " Cry out and shout, drink water, and praise the Lord."

Money soon poured in from all quarters : a shower of guineas. England is always ready to put her hand in her pocket when funds are needed for propagating a philanthropical or religious idea. Crowds of converts soon swelled the ranks ; little companies grew into big battalions ; and this association, which not long ago, had but a few hundred adherents in the country, has now grown to an army of four hundred thousand well disciplined soldiers, commanded by sergeants, lieutenants, captains and colonels, with a general at their head : the whole hierarchy.

The Salvation Army, intoxicated with success, continues its triumphal march from town to town, all through the country, and threatens to become a plague, neither more nor less. Not satisfied with holding its meetings in its barracks (this is the name given to their Bedlams, by these people), it sends detachments, headed by a band, to convert a certain neighbourhood, street or house. Woe betide you if your salvation should appear to some agent of the Salvation Army to be doubtful. A detachment will come and boldly plant itself under your windows, with trombones, cornets, tambourines and big drum, a cacophony fit to make your hair stand on end. "The devil is there ; let us fire a volley ! " they will cry, and whether you like it or not, you must be saved, unless you take the wise precaution of saving yourself, by flight. The police either dare not or will not interfere, and you have but one course open to you . it is to set aside the work you are engaged in, or the book you are reading, to go and soothe

the cries of your terrified baby, and just wait till these savages have bawled themselves hoarse, and retired.

The Salvation Army has its newspaper the *War Cry*, its head-quarters, its general staff, and, what is still more grave, its banker.

The different regiments receive their orders from the General in command. These proclamations, which are certainly a little blasphemous, are placarded about in public places. I will give you one or two. I copied the first at Scarborough.

"Captain Condy, the American tambourine player, and male and female warriors, with an army of blood and fire soldiers, will march through Scarborough to-day.

" At 6.30 a.m., knee-drill and handkerchief practice ; at 10.30 arrival of the Holy Ghost ; at 2.30 p.m., spiking of the enemy's cannon ; at 6.30, fire and blazes on the whole line ; at 8.30, Hallelujah gallop.

"On Monday, at 2.30 p.m., the American tambourinist will sing and speak in the name of Jesus, with other officers ; at 6.30 the soldiers will meet at the barracks for the PARADE, IN FULL UNIFORM : *red handkerchiefs, white jackets and aprons, and hallelujah bonnets compulsory.*

" Rebels will be offered conditions of peace.

"The surgeon of the army will attend to the wounded.

" By order of King Jesus and Captain Cadman."

I read the following placard at Torquay on regatta day in 1882 :—

"SALVATION ARMY.

"Gigantic meeting presided over by Major Pavey, Captain Davies, and Captain Harry.

"At 11 a.m. reception of the Holy Ghost.

"At noon, departure from the barracks, and triumphal march through the enemy's camp.

"At 2 p.m. a grand battle.

"A meeting in the fortress at 9.30 p.m. when red-hot gospel shots will be fired into the ranks of the devil's slaves." (By these latter are meant the harmless spectators of the races.)

"N.B.—A great surgeon (Jesus Christ) will be present to attend to the sick and wounded."

I one day went into one of the barracks of the Salvationists. The service was about to begin. The orchestra was composed of a trombone, two cornets, one tambourine, and two big drums. The latter instrument is the basis of all English music. I remember one day hearing the band of the first regiment of Royal Artillery play a fantasia on airs from the *Pré aux Clercs*. When they came to *Rendez-moi ma patrie*, the big drum struck up, and marked the time with formidable, emphatic strokes. To return to our heroes, they were yelling amid repeated rounds of applause an endless hymn, with the refrain, "Jesus is mine," when a fine fellow of about twenty years old stepped upon the platform, clapped his hands, and began turning round and round, till at last he fell senseless to the floor. The assembly rose to their feet as one man, and exclaimed: "He is saved! He is saved!"

"Not yet," cried a sceptic, who had taken up his

position near the door, all ready to decamp in case of necessity.

Thereupon another Salvationist began to pray: "Listen to the scoffers!" said he. "The devil is in our midst."

"The devil is in our midst!" repeated the assembly.

"Let us turn him out!" said the orator.

"Let us turn him out!" replied his hearers, with one voice.

The devil did not wait until a decision was arrived at. He made off without delay.

The wags are very annoying. I remember hearing one ask a pretty Salvationist if she felt saved. "What's that to you?" replied she. "Just hold your tongue, and mind your own business!"

The prayers at these meetings generally take the form of a litany: "O Lord, save the English nation, thy chosen people."

"Amen!" reply the congregation.

"Thou hast saved us, but there remain many yet who serve the devil; save them."

"Amen!"

And so on, until the resources of the orator's imagination are exhausted.

The numbers of the Salvationists and the banking account of the Army have attracted the attention of ecclesiastical authorities. And, indeed, there would be a nice little addition to be made to the revenues of the Anglican Church by admitting the Salvation

Army into its bosom. The Archbishop of Canterbury sent them five pounds towards the purchase of
barracks. The Queen herself went as far as to send
them her *moral support.* The Queen, as head of the
English Church, could not compromise herself by
making a present, which belonged by right to the
State Church. Besides, principles of economy are
known to be studied in the Royal Family.

Housekeepers begin to make bitter complaints
against the Army. Servants get restless; they feel
the need of being saved; and there is always a captain, or at least a sergeant, ready to lend a helping
hand.

I read in a police-court report the other day,
that a poor girl had been saved by a member of
the Salvation Army, who had taken her to his
lodgings in order to make more sure of success.
The saintly man had also robbed her of the few
trinkets she possessed. "Well!" as my missionary
friend remarked, "we are none of us perfect."

The *War Cry* announces the conversion of Jane
Johnson. It is a sad pity: the metropolis has thus
lost one of its most interesting types. Jane Johnson
is sixty-eight years of age, and has undergone two
hundred and ninety-six condemnations for drunkenness. In spite of the time she has spent in prison,
Jane, the champion drunkard of the world, enjoys
very good health, and there is every reason for be-
lieving that, had it not been for the deplorable in-
tervention of the Salvation Army, which cut short
her career in the prime of life, her end might have

been worthy of her life ; she might have died, as she had always lived, *ad majorem gloriam publicani.**

This grotesque state of things is the natural result of that constant splitting up into sects that the Reformed Church has undergone ever since the days of Cromwell. Many dissenting churches have set the example by vulgarising their services. They tried to make religion attractive, and they made it ludicrous. Ministers, transformed into actors, have been idolised, nay, almost worshipped, by congregations, who saw in them a Saviour, instead of lifting their eyes to Heaven. How many are there who would not go to church to worship God, but who go with willing feet to hear their dear minister? The original intention was good, but these performances have nevertheless helped to produce the results that I have attempted to describe in the present chapter.

One of the most eminent dissenting ministers—I might say the most eminent—took it into his head one day, in the midst of his sermon, to get astride the balusters of the pulpit staircase, and to let him-self glide to the foot of it. "There, my dear brethren," said he, on reappearing at the top, "that is how the wicked go down to hell." Titters, and almost applause, from the congregation.

I cannot take leave of the Salvation Army without saying a word or two about the General.

* At the moment of going to press, I hear with pleasure that Jane has just been condemned to eight days' imprisonment for her darling little failing. I am really glad of it : it would have been such a pity to spoil so interesting a career.

The Army recognises no authority but that of the General. He is all-powerful. He has the handling and management of the funds. He baptizes, marries, saves, or damns, the thousands of geese who obey his voice. The General's wife is as active as himself in the apostolic work that the family has undertaken. His sons and daughters are colonels, commanding detachments of the Army.

In the month of October, 1882, the General married his son to a young Salvationist. A large hall had been chosen for the occasion, and the price of admission fixed at a shilling. The iron must be struck while it is hot: who knows how long the temporary insanity of the Salvationists will last?

The hall was thronged; the young couple were blessed beyond the hopes of the General and his family. Six thousand persons at a shilling each, that made three hundred pounds.

The General is no fool.

I cannot imagine why, in this country, where advertising is so successful, the General has not yet invented a celestial mixture, or salvation pills. Salvation pills! What a tremendous success they would have! The General might insert in the *War Cry* testimonials something in the style of the following.

"Dear General,—On Saturday night I took one of your marvellous—I should say miraculous—pills. I went to bed a hardened sinner: I woke up converted. A few more pills, and I shall be a saint. Every one ought to have some of these pills in his bedroom. You may make what use you please

15

of this letter. I enclose a P.O.O. for two and six, and beg you to send me a box of salvation pills for my wife."

A peculiar faith is the faith of the Peculiar People. So great is their faith in God that, when any of the fraternity fall ill, no doctor is called to their bedside, because, say they, to call in a doctor is to insult God and prove that you have no confidence in Him. "If it is the Lord's will that I should die, let His will be done. Nothing can save me ; if it is His will that I should recover, then He can save me without the help of any doctor."

I could not better describe to you the religious opinions of the sect, which, by the way, has numerous followers, than by giving you an extract from the account of a trial, at which a father was accused of having caused the death of his child by negligence.

Magistrate.—"Your child died. You refused to send for a doctor, did you not?"

Prisoner.—"It was the Lord's will that he should die, no doctor could have saved him."

Magistrate.—"But when you saw your child was dangerously ill, do you not think it was your duty to have called in a doctor?"

Prisoner.—"No, I fear the Lord, and place my trust in Him."

Magistrate.—"But suppose, for instance, that you were run over by a carriage and had your leg broken, would you not send for the doctor?"

Prisoner.—"Such a thing could not happen to

me. God protects me, and He has said that not a bone of the just shall be broken."

Magistra. e.—" But supposing they should break ?"

Prisoner.—" It is impossible to suppose it."

Magistrate—" I respect all religious opinions. But once more, do you not consider that you ought to have called in medical aid, when you saw your child's life in danger ? "

Prisoner.—" No. If God had not been willing that he should die, he could not have died. Ah ! gentlemen of the jury, if you really believed in God, you would not allow such questions to be put to me. When we have a sick person in our houses, we anoint him with oil, and we pray according to the command given us in the Epistle of St. James. If God is pleased to take him from us, we submit ourselves to His divine will."

The whole account of the case appeared in the newspapers of the 24th January, 1883.

Two months later, the same man was prosecuted for having allowed a second child to die under the same circumstances.

After all, I do not know that there is anything very extraordinary in this belief, for such a free and free-trading people as the English. A medical student, who cannot obtain his diploma by examination in England, has only to go to Scotland to obtain one without difficulty, or to America to buy one. There are plenty of people ready to trust their friends in his hands. This being so, it is not very wonderful that there should be others to be found who prefer trusting to Providence.

There arose in Devonshire, in the early part of the century, a religious sect named the Jumpers. Its originator was Joanna Southcott, a woman who gave out that she was possessed by the spirit of the Virgin Mary. The doctrine she taught was intended to prove that the devil is everywhere, and that Christians should jump upon him. The higher they jumped, the more heavily they would come down on him, and the more chance they had of being saved. The devil did not enjoy life just then, I can assure you. These worthy folks had their chapels, where they jumped to their hearts' content, without uttering a word. The Jumpers have not yet altogether disappeared. At one time, Joanna Southcott believed herself to be *enciente*, by the Holy Spirit. Her followers made great preparations for the worthy reception of the Holy Child that was expected. Unhappily they were disappointed ; Joanna died and carried her secret with her to the tomb. The Southcottians, who believe Joanna to be no other than the woman of the desert spoken of by St. John in the Book of Revelation, still look for her resurrection. Good luck to them !

XXXI.

The English Nation no other than the Lost Ten Tribes of Israel—
The Anglo-Israel Identity Society—Seventy-seven Proofs of
Identity—Tender-handed, touch the nettle, and it stings you
for your pains ; grasp it like a man of mettle, and it soft as silk
remains—Wanted more Missionaries—A New Proof of Identity.

BROUGHT up in the Bible, the English nation must
have had all its sympathies enlisted on behalf of that
nation, ungrateful, cowardly and bloodthirsty, but
chosen of God, before whom the walls of besieged
towns fell at sound of trumpets, to whom the Lord
spoke in person, and for whom he fought by show-
ering hailstones on their enemies.

At the destruction of Jerusalem, the Jews were
dispersed : I mean the Jews of the tribes of Judah
and Levi, otherwise called the children of the House
of Judah. The other ten tribes, that is to say, the
children of Israel, were lost sight of entirely, and
historians have never been able to discover a trace
of them.

John Bull, who attributes his successes in this
world to his superiority to all other nations in religious matters, said to himself : " Who knows ? might
I not be the lost child of Israel ? "

" It is certain that I do great things, that I am the
Elect of Heaven by special appointment ; is it not
just possible that he who commanded the sun to

stand still was an ancestor of mine ? " And so, he
tried to identify himself with that people who
crossed the Red Sea without wetting the sole of their
feet.

A society has been formed, in England, under the
name of the " Anglo-Israel Identity Society," with
the object of proving that the inhabitants of Great
Britain are none other than the lost ten tribes of the
House of Israel. This Society has not been idle : up
to the present time, it has discovered no fewer than
seventy-seven proofs, all taken from Scripture, of the
identity in question. About a hundred books and
pamphlets upon the subject have been published,
adherents have thronged in, and the nation need no
longer be surprised at its successes ; the finger of
God is in its work.

These proofs of identity are rather clever. I will
give you a few.

" *The children of Israel were to inhabit islands lying
north-west from Palestine, and to speak a language that
was not Hebrew.*

" The English inhabit islands ; those islands lie
north-west from Palestine, and their language is composed of about 43,000 words of Latin, Germanic, or
Celtic origin.

" The Semitic element is absent.

" *Israel was to possess colonies in all parts of the
earth.*"

Thus do they interpret the third verse of Isaiah
(liv.): " Thou shall break forth on the right hand,
and on the left, and thy seed shall inherit the Gen-
tiles and make the desolate cities to be inhabited."

I must quote a few extracts from the pamphlets of the Society. It is doing a great deal of honour to such writings to reproduce them, even in such an unpretentious book as this, but it is interesting to show to what a pitch stupidity can be carried, when national vanity and religious mania have a hand in the matter.

"Whether we desire it or not, we must possess colonies; it is our destiny. The Dutch and the Spaniards have had colonies and lost them, almost all, what paltry ones they have must soon cede away from them. The French virtually have none. The Germans have tried and failed; but the British nation has flourishing colonies in all parts of the world, and urgently requires more yet. The Turkish Empire is on the eve of ruin, and as Constantinople will be ours by right, we shall have to take immediate possession of it. Constantinople is the very gate of highway to our largest and best foreign possession —India, with her teeming millions and her forty distinct languages."

"*Israel must have a nation from her, but independent of her.*"

"There is much reason to thank God," says one of these productions, "that America can celebrate year by year her Declaration of Independence."

Again: "America is a great nation; hallelujah! it was ordained that she should separate herself from us."

Jonathan succeeded, in 1776, in sending John Bull about his business *vi et armis;* and the result is, that John has the greatest respect for him; he never

loses an opportunity of whispering a flattering word
in his ear.

> " Tender-handed, touch the nettle,
>   And it stings you for your pains ;
>   Grasp it like a man of mettle,
>   And it soft as silk remains."

" *Israel must now be under a monarchy.*"

I will admit that no monarchy appears to me to be
so firmly established as that of England.

" *Israel cannot be conquered in their isles, and must
conquer against all odds.*"

"The French, the Russians, the Spanish, the Dutch,
the Chinese, the Indians, the Germans, the Austrians,
and the Italians, cannot any of them be Israel, because they have been defeated."

" The British alone have never been defeated ;
ergo, they must be Israel."

This trash is printed, at the author's expense I
need not tell you, but, however, printed it is.

I will quote again :

"We are the only nation that can dare to face
fearful odds. This seal of Identity with Israel was
verified in the Peninsular War, when the Duke of
Wellington withstood, by a small army, nearly the
entire forces of the continent." (Do not stare with in-
credulity ; it is all written down in plain characters :
I have not imagination enough to write history in such
a style as that, believe me.)   " We withstood the peo·
ple of China, computed by millions, with only a few
boat-loads of men, and prevailed against them ! We
hold India, with her teeming millions, under the

power of a few white men. We prevailed against
Russia at the Crimea, with but a very small force.
(Not one word about the two hundred thousand poor
fools of Frenchmen that were there, to say nothing
of the forty thousand Turks.) And our victories
over the Ashantees, the Afghans, the Zulus, and the
Egyptians! If they had all to be counted we should
never have done." Nevertheless let us have done
quickly, with your consent; it is sickening. The
preceding lines have been extracted, however, from
one of the most *serious* books, published under the
auspices of the Society : *ex uno disce omnes*. In making its lists of victorious campaigns, you may notice
that the Society has prudently omitted to mention
that of the Transvaal. The fact of the Boers having
given John a sound thrashing, would naturally have
made it a little less easy to establish the thirty-third
proof of identity. The sturdy Boers are now masters in their own country, and modern Israel never
mentions them, except with the greatest respect.

" *Israel must be a Sabbath-keeping people.*"

"Ah!" cries the Identity Society, "is not our
metropolis a sign, a wonder, and an astonishment
each recurring Sabbath to every foreigner who visits
our shores? it is indeed a sublime spectacle. Four
millions of the busiest population of the world vol-
untarily close almost every house of business, almost
every place of public amusement or of recreation,
cutting themselves off from the surrounding world
for twenty-four hours. Post-offices completely shut,
telegraphs and railways all but standing still, the
vast majority of the citizens rest from the labours of

the week ; and why ?—LONDON KEEPETH SABBATH.⁴
This is not exact: the provinces have their Sunday
post ; telegrams can be sent on Sundays ; and the
London trains are only stopped during the hours of
morning service.   The public-houses remain open,
and it is well known that there are more burglaries
committed on Sundays than on any other day.   It
would appear that the House of Israel does not rest
so completely on the Sabbath as the Society would
have us believe.

" *Israel shall be a prolific race.*"

God did indeed promise Abraham that he should
be the father of multitudes, that his descendants
should be as numerous as the stars of the heaven.
Jacob, in his dream, was told by the Lord that he
should possess the ground upon which he reposed
and that his children should be as the dust of the
earth.

" Where is there to be found," says the Society,
"a nation that multiplies as rapidly as the British ?"

It is a fact that the Anglo-Saxon races, at the rate
at which they are multiplying at present, will, in
the year 2,000, number 1,837 millions.   The *Quar-*
terly Scientific Review for the month of June, 1873,
tells us that the Anglo-Saxons double their population, in Europe, in fifty-six years ; in the colonies, in
twenty-five years ; whilst the Germans take a hundred, and the French a hundred and forty years to
double theirs.

Ergo, England must be Israel.

" What a number of children you have in this
country !" I remarked one day to an Englishman.

"Well, you see," he replied, "we have so few other distractions!"

"The House of Israel shall send missionaries to the ends of the earth."

This proof is taken from the Bible (Isa. xliii. 21): "This people have I formed for Myself: they shall show forth My praise." England sends missionaries to all parts of the world; but these commercial travellers of the Bible Society, excellent political agents, I must say, are unfortunately sent to the wrong address: they go where their services are not required.

De cette vérité deux fables feront foi :

In the colony of Natal, a Zulu sold a Christian a tough fowl. A few days after, the latter complained. What did the savage do? He gave the white man another fowl and refused his money.

I know an Englishman, whose name is Legion, who bought of a London poulterer an old rook that had been recommended to him as a tender young chicken fresh from Devonshire. What did the civilised man do? Knowing the poulterer to be no Zulu, he made the best of his bad bargain and broken teeth.

Why do not the missionaries all stay in London? What a splendid field for their labours!

Can it be thou, O Israel, chosen child of the Lord, who hast changed the standard weight of the sanctuary into a *bonne à tout faire?* Change thy shouts of joy into bitter lamentations, O Jerusalem!

There can be no more doubt upon the subject Lost Israel has been found. The proofs are irre. futable.

If I might be permitted to contribute to the work already done by the Society, I should like to add one more proof, which appears to me to be conclusive. The house of Judah was told : " Behold, My servants shall drink, but ye shall be thirsty " (Isa. lxv. 13).

I find in an official report, got up by the English Government in 1877, that the number of persons arrested for drunkenness in England alone that is to say, without counting Scotland and Ireland, where tippling is quite as popular as in England, was, in the year 1876, no less than 104,174. Out of this number 38,880 were women ; and since the year 1876 these ugly figures have not diminished.

If you consider that the number of drunkards arrested in the street for disorderly conduct only represent a very small portion of the persons addicted to drink, since there is no law to prevent any one from getting intoxicated in his own house, and the drunkards arrested are only those who are utterly helpless, or who cause disorder in the streets, you will be convinced that, to employ the style of the Society, since the British nation alone can produce such figures, *ergo* she must be Israel.*

---

* This new proof of mine has been pronounced so irrefutable by my friends that they expect to see me elected a Fellow of the Society very shortly.

XXXII.

To sum up in a few words—

The Englishman is more earnest than we are ; his judgment is more sound, more healthy, more unimpassioned than ours ; and his patriotism more intelligent. Cold in manner, sober and quiet by temperament, of a shy and melancholy disposition, brought up in the crude training of the Bible, and in an austere religion that implants in him almost a dread of joy and happiness, the Englishman is less lovable and less happy than ourselves.

Education, climate, and food, all help to account for the striking difference that exists between the English and French characters. The man, whose dinner consists of a pound of beef, a large slice of plum pudding, and a tankard of thick, heavy, black beer, must certainly look at things in a different light from the man who dines off oysters, chicken, fruit, the lightest of pastry, and a bottle of Pomard.

I was speaking one day, in the presence of a few Englishmen, of the sorry face that one of the greatest French statesmen of the age exhibited at his window, between two tapers, on an evening of public rejoicing. "Ha!" they cried, in chorus, "you will admit that no Englishman would do such a thing as that."

"You are right," I replied, "the climate would not allow it."

In this country of contrasts, where, on the one hand, you have such high morality, and on the other hand such dark and deep-rooted vice, you are tempted to wonder how it is that the English are not Manichæans. It really seems as if dualism must preside over the destinies of England; there need be no hesitation in affirming that in this country good and evil are greater than in France,—a judgment which M. Taine pronounces, though timidly.

We are constantly accusing England of being selfish in her policy. But is not patriotism the most manifest and excusable form of selfishness? Is it selfishness to prefer one's mother to any other woman? Is it selfishness to think one's children handsomer and more intelligent than those of other people? Is it selfishness to accept a good situation, rather than refuse it and offer it, like a good Christian, to one's neighbour? Show me a country that opens its doors more hospitably and generously to the foreigner. Show me another country where he meets with so much attention and respect. All that is required of him is that he shall respect the law; and, short of being able to sit in Parliament, he enjoys all the privileges of a born Englishman.

John Bull's patriotism is intelligent. As a man of business, he never enters into the perils of a war, unless he is pretty sure of benefiting himself in some way ; and the Continental Powers, who keep up great standing armies at an enormous expense, to acquire in return nothing but a little glory, are jealous, and grumble. In the year 1878, at the time when England and Russia were shaking their fists at each other, I read in a newspaper that a Russian coachman, discovering one day that he was driving an English fare, politely begged him to alight, and indignantly refused the money that was offered to him. Now this is not patriotism, as John Bull understands it. A London cabman, under similar circumstances, would have doubled his charge.

M. Alexis de Tocqueville has drawn a portrait of the Frenchman that appears to me to be hit off to the life. "Worshipping hazard, power, success, brilliancy, and fame, more than true glory," says this great writer ; "more capable of heroism than of virtue, of genius than of good sense ; with more aptitude for conceiving immense designs than for carrying through great enterprises ; the most brilliant nation in Europe, and the best calculated to become in turn an object of admiration, of hatred, of pity, of terror, but of indifference--never !" On the contrary, the Englishman has greatness, but no magnanimity ; virtue, but no heroism when British interests are not at stake. He is not so brilliant or so impulsive as his neighbour more richly endowed by Nature, but he is more independent, more enterprising, more persevering, and more wise.

France and England together would seem to unite in themselves all the qualities that intelligence and industry can develop, and the union of these two great nations, which, under the reign of a virtuous queen, has been steadily growing more and more perfect, justifies the hope that only in the arts of peace will they ever again be rivals ; and that, hand in hand, they will ever be found mutually encouraging each other in the path of progress and liberty.

Let us conclude by quoting Voltaire's saying : " If I had had to choose my birthplace, I would have chosen England."

APPENDIX.

(A.)—At Devon Assizes (April, 1883), a convict was tried for maliciously wounding with intent to kill a warder of the Dartmoor prison. The deputy-governor of Dartmoor prison was called, and said that when the prisoner was brought to him, he asked him if he had anything to say for himself, upon which the prisoner replied that he did not care if he swung for it.

Prisoner (interrupting).—"I do not remember saying that to you."

Governor.—"That only proves what an unmitigated liar you are."

Judge (to witness).—"You are here to give evidence, and not to insult the prisoner, whom it is my duty to protect."

Governor.—"My lord, the prisoner is one of the worst characters in the prison."

Judge (to witness).—"If I hear you make another statement against the prisoner extra-judicially, I shall mark my opinion of it in a very decided manner. We are here to try the prisoner, not upon his antecedents, but upon the facts. . . . I am astonished that the deputy-governor should have used

such observations for the purpose of prejudicing
the prisoner's case.   It was discreditable to him as
an official, and disgraceful to him as a gentleman
and a man.   I must caution the jury not to let the
disgust which they may feel at that attempt lead
them into a wrong direction to a feeling of sympathy with the prisoner.   The foolish and wicked observations of the deputy-governor will certainly not
have the effect he intended."

The jury, however, found the prisoner guilty, and
he was sentenced to fifteen years' penal servitude.

(B.)—Eleven criminals were hanged in England,
Scotland, and Ireland, during the month of May,
1883.

The following words are extracted from a speech
of Mr. John Bright, delivered in May, 1883 :—

" But to show how little influence the Christian
Church, the Church of England, had with the Government of our country in these matters, let me tell
you that up to the reign of George the First,
there were in this country sixty-seven offences that
were punishable with death.   Between the accession
of George the First and the termination of the
reign of George the Third—I think within those
limits—there were added 156 new crimes to which
the capital punishment was attached.   Now during
all these years, as far as this question goes, our Government was becoming more cruel and more barbarous,—(hear, hear)—and we did not find, and have
not found, that in the great Church of England,
with its ten, fifteen, or twenty thousand ministers,
and with its more than a score of bishops in the

House of Lords, there ever seems to have been a voice raised or an organization formed in favour of a more merciful code, or any condemnation of the enormous cruelty which our law was continually inflicting. (Hear, hear.) Was not Voltaire justified in saying that the English were the only people who murdered by law ? (Hear, hear.) "

THE END.